The secu.....

IMITATION & ALCHEMY

All Ben Vecchio wanted was a quiet summer before his last semester of university. Was that too much to ask?

All Tenzin wanted was a cache of priceless medieval coins that had been missing for several hundred years.

And some company.

Phrases like "never again" don't mean much when you've been a vampire for several thousand years. And promises made in the heat of anger don't always outweigh the lure of gold. Ben Vecchio thought he knew everything there was to know about the immortals of Italy. But when Tenzin tempts him into another adventure, finding a cache of rare gold coins missing since the nineteenth century, he'll discover that familiar places can hold the most delicious secrets. And possibly the key to his future.

Ben and Tenzin are back in an all-new novella in the Elemental Legacy series.

Imitation
& ALCHEMY

An Elemental Legacy Novella

ELIZABETH HUNTER

Imitation and Alchemy
Copyright © 2015
Elizabeth Hunter
ISBN: 978-1519741318

This is a work of fiction. Names, characters, places, and incidents are the products of the author's imagination or are used fictitiously. Any resemblance to actual persons, living or dead, business establishments, events, or locales is entirely coincidental.

Cover artist: Damonza.com
Developmental Editor: Lora Gasway
Copy Editor: Anne Victory
Formatter: Elizabeth Hunter

Elizabeth Hunter
PO Box 8085
Visalia, CA 93290
U.S.A.

THIS BOOK IS DEDICATED TO
MY ONGOING LOVE AFFAIR WITH ITALY.

And to all my readers who love it too.

Prologue

BENJAMIN VECCHIO SAT IN THE library of his home in Pasadena, studying for his art history final. To say the class was an easy A would be a gross understatement, but the habits instilled by his scholar of an uncle wouldn't allow him to rest for the night until he'd at least looked over his notes.

A small air vampire floated into the room and over the library table, blocking his notebook. She settled on his textbook and waited silently for Ben to acknowledge her.

He glanced up at Tenzin a second before he shook his head. "Nope."

She said nothing, watching Ben with storm-grey eyes that always seemed just a little out of place. Her features were unquestionably born on the steppes of Central Asia. Her full lips remained closed over the lethal, clawlike fangs in her mouth. And her expression? It revealed nothing.

"Whatever it is," he continued, "the answer is no. I can't spar tonight. I have a final tomorrow. And I don't have time to get online and research an obscure manuscript in Sanskrit or whatever it is you want. I need to sleep."

The air vampire continued to watch him silently. Ben

continued to ignore her. Ignoring Tenzin when she wanted something from him was a talent he'd been honing for years.

She had a face that could have been fifteen or thirty, depending on her expression. She'd let her hair grow out to below her shoulders the past few years, so she looked younger than Ben now. If you didn't know who or what she was, she could pass herself off as an innocent schoolgirl.

Well, until she smiled and you saw the fangs.

She used her looks to her advantage, but no matter what expression Tenzin wore, Ben saw millennia when he looked into her eyes.

She ignored his indifference and leaned over his notes. "Why are you studying this? You knew about neoclassicism before I met you."

He grimaced. Modern universities were inexplicable to Tenzin. "I need the credits if I'm going to graduate next winter. I only have one more semester, and I've ignored most of my lower-level requirements."

"Because they are stupid."

"Art history is not stupid."

She flicked the edge of his notebook. "Taking a class where you probably know more than the instructor is stupid."

"Well, they wouldn't let me take the upper-level class."

"Why not?"

"Because I hadn't taken the lower level... Listen"—he sat back in his chair—"do you have a purpose here? What do you want?"

"It doesn't matter." She shrugged. "You've already said no."

"Tenzin—"

"Why are you taking art history?" She stretched out on the table, lazing like a cat. "What does art history have to do with political science?"

"Nothing. It's just part of my— Will you get off that?" He pulled his textbook from under her hair. "I need to study—"

"No, you don't! You've known art since you were old enough to steal it. Do you want some food? I feel like cooking. What would you like? I'll cook food and you can eat it."

"What do you want, Tenzin?"

She rolled over and propped her chin on her hands; her eyes laughed at him. "You already said no."

"Just tell me."

She kicked her legs. "I want to go to Italy this summer."

His eye twitched and he looked back to his book. "No."

"You go to Italy all the time."

"I learned my lesson last summer, Tiny."

"We're not going to China. I want to go to Italy. It's practically a second home to you. You have a house in Rome."

"*Gio* has a house in Rome. If you want to borrow it, ask him."

"You speak Italian like a native. You have friends

there. You could visit Fabia."

"Fabia has a boyfriend lately."

"So?"

"Just... no."

She didn't move from her position stretched on the table. Not even when he picked up his notes and stood them up, blocking her face.

"What if—"

"No!" He slammed his notebook down. "No. No. No. I'm not getting involved in one of your schemes. I'm not stealing anything. I'm not pretending to be your butler again—"

"I only told one person that, and I think Jonathan knew it was a joke."

"I do not want to lie to dangerous people. I don't want to run for my life. I don't want to hurt anyone. I don't want to get beat up or threatened or—"

"Fine!" She scowled and lay on her back, huffing at the ceiling. "What happened to you? You used to be fun."

"I grew up, Tenzin. And I realized that I can't live in my aunt and uncle's house forever. I'm twenty-two. I'm going to have to get a job one of these days. And a house. And pay bills." Ben grimaced. "I'm going to have to figure out something useful to do with my life, and I have no idea what the hell that means for someone like me."

He slammed his notes back on the table and tried to concentrate, all the while feeling her eyes on him like a brand.

After a few minutes, she crawled across the table and leaned down to his ear. Tenzin whispered, "Medieval

4

gold coins from Sicily."

He groaned and let his head fall back. "I hate you a little right now."

– ⊕ –

GIOVANNI was in the den, curled up with a book, Beatrice lying across his legs while she caught a movie.

Ben stopped in the doorway and watched them.

It was a hell of a lot to aspire to. Some days his heart ached watching them. As much as they loved him—and he knew his aunt and uncle loved him a lot—the love they had for each other was so tangible it almost hurt. He couldn't imagine having love like that. If he ever did, he'd grab on to it with everything he had.

Ben would never forget the months they spent in Rome when he was sixteen. When Giovanni had been taken, leaving Beatrice alone. It was the first time he ever remembered feeling stronger than his aunt.

Giovanni looked up with a smile. "Hello."

"Hey."

Beatrice stretched her legs and kicked a pillow off the end of the couch. "What are you doing tonight? Come sit with us."

Ben walked over and sat down. "I was just studying. Two more finals before summer break."

Beatrice smiled. "I'm so proud of you. Have I told you that lately? We're both so proud of you. I can't believe you've almost earned your degree."

He glanced at their loving smiles before he turned

away in embarrassment. "Thanks."

Beatrice was thirty-eight now but looked barely older than Ben.

It was odd to realize that in a few years he would be the one who looked older than his aunt. Their relationship was already changing, becoming more friendly than parental. Just another reminder that time was passing.

Too fast, a childish voice whispered inside. *Too fast!*

"What do you think you want to do this summer?" Giovanni asked. "You should do something fun. Beatrice and I are stuck here, working on that damned library theft." He added a string of Latin curses that had Beatrice smoothing her thumb over his lips.

"Shhhh," she said. "You'll shock the boy."

"I don't think that's possible anymore," Giovanni said.

Ben had forgotten all about the library heist when he was thinking about how to sneak off to Italy without his uncle becoming suspicious.

It had been a massive scandal in the rare-book world and had become the bane of his uncle's existence since much of the "uncatalogued special collections" that had been stolen from the Girolamini Library in Naples wasn't actually part of the library but was instead the private collections of numerous Italian immortals. Some of the vampires had stored their private miscellany in the library since the sixteenth century and did not take kindly to humans stealing and selling their treasured manuscripts or personal papers.

Giovanni and Beatrice had been hired by multiple clients to track down particularly elusive items that had made their way onto the black market. The Naples library heist had been keeping them—along with their resident librarians in Perugia, Zeno and Serafina—busy on and off for almost two years.

Ben cleared his throat. "It's funny you mentioned Naples. I was actually thinking of going to Italy for part of my break."

Beatrice frowned. "In the summer? But it's so hot! You sure you don't want to go down to Chile?"

"I haven't seen my friends there since Christmas. And Fabi's seeing a guy she wanted me to meet. So—"

"The house in Rome is yours anytime you want," Giovanni said. "You know that. In fact..." He frowned. "If you don't mind doing some work while you're there, I think Zeno will be in Rome the middle of June working at the Vatican Library. I might have you take some notes to him."

"And that journal we tracked down in New York last month," Beatrice said. "Ben can take that to Zeno too. Collect on that commission."

"Good idea, Tesoro," he murmured, brushing her dark hair from her cheek. "Ben, let me know if you want to borrow the plane. But right now—"

"Got it." He stood when he saw Beatrice turning to her mate. "I know when I'm not wanted."

"Close the door on the way out."

Glancing over his shoulder, Ben saw Giovanni had already pulled Beatrice to straddle him. He tried not to laugh.

Like rabbits, the two of them.

"Ben—" Giovanni pulled his lips from his mate's and cleared his throat. "I'll let Emil know you'll be in Rome this summer. You know the game. Just make sure you stay out of Naples."

Ben's Tenzin-radar went off. Naples. Southern Italy. Sicily. Very southern Italy...

Medieval *Sicilian* coins, huh?

"What's up with Naples?" he asked, trying to sound casual. "Problems with the VIC?"

"The 'vampire in charge' as you say, is named Alfonso. He's Spanish. Or Hungarian. I'm not sure. And he's..." Giovanni frowned.

"He's nuts," Beatrice threw out. "Completely bonkers. And mean. He hates Emil."

"Ah." Ben nodded. "Big Livia supporter?"

Beatrice said, "No, he hated Livia too."

Giovanni was watching his mate with the focused stare that told Ben he'd forgotten anyone but Beatrice was in the room. It was the vampire hunting stare, and Ben knew if he didn't get out of the den quickly, he was going to see way more of his aunt and uncle than he wanted.

"Just..." Beatrice held Giovanni back. "Stay out of Naples. It's not a good idea right now. The rest of the country? No problem."

"Avoid Naples." He gave them a thumbs-up they probably didn't see. "Got it. Later. Don't do anything I wouldn't do. Except, you know, the biting stuff I don't

8

want to know about."

"Good night, Benjamin."

He shut the double doors behind him and leaned back, letting out a long breath before he walked to his bedroom. "How much you want to bet...?"

– ⊕ –

THE next night, he was working with Tenzin at her warehouse in East Pasadena. She'd converted most of the old building to a training area, complete with one full wall of weapons. The only personal space was a loft in the rafters with no ground access.

Because the only person allowed up there could fly.

The windows were blacked out, which made life easier when you didn't sleep. At all. Ben didn't know how she stayed sane. Then again, the state of Tenzin's sanity was never a settled subject.

"Look at that." She leaned over his shoulder and reached her finger toward the computer screen, which began to flicker before he slapped her hand away.

"Don't touch."

They were watching a video about Kalaripayattu, an obscure Indian martial art, that someone had posted on YouTube. Tenzin *adored* YouTube.

"But look at those forms," she said. "So much similarity to modern yoga. But more..."

"Martial."

"Yes, exactly. If you could isolate pressure points..."

She started muttering in her own language, which no

one but Tenzin and her sire spoke anymore, though Ben thought he was starting to pick up some words. Giovanni theorized it was a proto-Mongolian dialect of some kind, but Ben only spoke Mandarin. He hadn't delved into Central or Northern Asian languages yet.

"If you watch..." She frowned. "The balance. That is key. This is very good. We'll incorporate some of the balance exercises for you since you are top-heavy now."

"It's called muscular, and it's a product of testosterone. I refuse to apologize for that."

"Look." She slapped his arm. "The short-stick fighting. We can incorporate some of those techniques too."

"Are you saying I have a short stick?"

She frowned, still staring at the computer screen. "What are you talking about?"

Ben tried to stifle a smile. She could be so adorably clueless for a woman with thousands of years behind her. "Nothing. Ignore me."

"Oh!" She laughed. "Was that a sexual joke? That was funny. But your stick is not short, Benjamin." She patted his arm. "You have nothing to be worried about."

"Thanks. That's... comforting." He cleared his throat. "So, I told Gio I was heading to Italy for the summer. He said the house in Rome is mine as long as I help Zeno out with some stuff at the Vatican while I'm there."

"That's good." She cocked her head, her eyes still stuck on the video playing. "Can you skip ahead to the dagger fighting?"

"Yeah." He found the section that was her favorite. "So, Tiny, when you said that we'd be looking for Sicilian coins, did you mean we'll be going to Sicily?"

"Don't be ridiculous," she said, leaning closer to the screen. "We're going to Naples. That's where the gold is. Or where it was."

"Of course it is."

"Is Naples going to be a problem?"

"With you, Tenzin?" Ben leaned back and crossed his arms. "There's really no way of knowing."

Chapter One

BEN FELT HIS SHOULDERS RELAX as soon as he stepped into the terminal of Leonardo da Vinci International Airport. He walked quickly through the crowd, making his way past the slow-moving early-summer tourists. He'd skipped a checked suitcase—the notes and journal Giovanni had given him were wrapped in the bottom of his messenger bag—so if he timed things right...

He arrived at passport control just before an enormous tour group of Chinese visitors flooded the line. With a few quick stamps and another few rote questions, the girl checking his passport stamped it and waved him through.

"*Benvenuto a Roma, Signor Vecchio.*"

"*Grazie. Ciao.*"

With his name and near-impeccable accent, she probably figured Ben for an Italian despite his American passport.

It wouldn't be far off.

Though his blood was an even mix between Puerto Rican and Lebanese, he could easily pass for an Italian, especially when he grew out his beard, which he'd done as soon as his semester had ended.

Slipping on his sunglasses, Ben grabbed a cab and

relaxed into the backseat, letting out a long breath as the taxi wound its way through the traffic of midday Rome. The driver hummed along with the quick jazz on the radio but didn't try to talk to him. Ben gave him an address near the Pantheon and leaned back to close his eyes.

Rome.

Ben smiled. It was good to be back.

Home had always been a fluid concept to Ben. It consisted far more of the people present than any particular location. Home was Giovanni and Beatrice. Caspar and Isadora. Dez and Matt. But home was also Angela, Giovanni's longtime housekeeper in Rome. If there was any city that felt more like home than Los Angeles, it was probably Rome. Some of his happiest and most terrible memories were here.

He started awake from his snooze when the driver stopped in the tiny Piazza di Santa Chiara. Ben paid him and grabbed his bag, then waited for the driver to pull away before he made his way up the side street that led to the house.

After punching in the code for the giant wooden door that shielded the property from prying eyes, he pulled it open, wondering how Angela was coping with the gate when she ran errands. His uncle, being a five-hundred-year-old vampire, tended to forget about things like human frailties and arthritis.

"*Ciao*, Angela!" he called into the courtyard.

He heard a fluttering like bird wings before a tiny woman appeared from the kitchen on the ground floor.

"*Ciao, Nino!*" Angela covered his cheeks with her small, wrinkled hands and pulled him down for a kiss, chattering as he laughed.

Angela had to be in her late sixties, but she still had the bright eyes and impeccable style of a woman much younger. She'd run Giovanni's house in Rome for most of her adult life with a healthy balance of efficiency, warmth, and Tuscan comfort food.

"You've gotten taller since Christmas," she said.

"No. I promise I haven't." He'd filled out a bit in the shoulders, but he was done growing. Almost six feet would have to suffice.

"You're too thin!" She pinched his arm. "Nino, what do they feed you in California? It's not enough. Come." She waved him into the kitchen. "I'm making meatballs for you and Fabi for dinner."

He rubbed his eyes. Now that he was within the familiar walls of Residenza di Spada, he felt the delayed exhaustion hit. He'd bypassed the offer of Giovanni's plane, choosing to use some of his frequent-flyer miles to upgrade to first class, but he hadn't really slept for almost twenty-four hours.

"Angie, I think I might lie down for a little bit."

"Not too long!" The housekeeper was accustomed to international guests. "Sleep for a little. I'll wake you up for dinner. You need to get on Roman time."

"*Sì, zia.*"

"Your room is made up. Fresh sheets on the bed and I washed the clothes you left here. Not many summer things, I don't think."

Because he usually avoided the furnace of Rome in the summer. He could already feel his shirt sticking to his back. "I'll be fine. I'll pick up some new things tomorrow."

At least there was no lack of shopping in Rome. It was expensive, but Ben thought the quality was worth the extra cash, and he saved most of his formal shopping for Italian visits.

He walked upstairs and tucked Giovanni's notes and the journal in the safe in the master suite, then made his way to the cool shadows of his room where he toppled face-first into bed.

– ⊕ –

SHE was playing with the curls of his hair when he woke. Soft humming and the warm smell of citrus and bergamot she'd worn since she was a teenager. Ben rolled over and grabbed Fabia around the waist.

"Gotcha," he said, his voice still rough with sleep.

Fabia laughed as she fell against his chest.

"Bad boy," she said, brushing a kiss against his jaw. "The beard is so sexy. I love your hair longer. You should always wear it that way."

Ben lay back, her familiar weight resting against his body. He took a deep breath and let his fingers trail over her smooth shoulders as Fabi laid her head on his chest and hugged him.

Women were just so... delicious.

Other than friendly kisses and a few teenage

fumblings, he and Angie's niece had never been more than friends, but the flirtation of more had always lain between them. Fabia was a beautiful girl. Smart and effortlessly sexy. She'd shorn her red-brown hair into a pixie cut when she entered her graduate program and moved to Rome. It suited her.

"I missed you," she said.

"Why did you get a boyfriend then?" He smiled at her when she looked up. "I can't kiss you—well, I can't kiss you as much—if you have a boyfriend."

"I don't want a boyfriend who lives in California most of the year." She pouted. "I am not made for a long-distance lover, Ben."

"You could move to LA."

"And you could move to Rome."

They both grinned at the same time.

Ah well. Not meant to be, no matter how the chemistry taunted them.

He leaned down, gave her a quick kiss, then rolled her to the side while he went to use the attached bath.

"So how hot is it?" he asked through the door as he splashed water on his face and pulled off his sweat-stained shirt.

"Not too bad yet," she said. "But July is just around the corner."

He walked out and caught her admiring his bare chest with an arched eyebrow.

"I don't have many clothes," he said. "I'll need to go shopping."

"I can go with you tomorrow." She sat up and went

to the wardrobe, opening it and surveying the contents with a frown. "You're right." She threw a shirt at him and closed the doors. "Wear that for dinner. It'll do. We're meeting some friends tonight by the river."

"Is the fair going on?"

"*Sul Lungotevere,*" she said. "Good restaurants this year."

During the summer, the banks of the Tiber were taken over by restaurants and vendors who took advantage of the cool evenings to lure locals and tourists to the river. It was a combination of food, drink, and art that Fabi had told him about, but he'd never had a chance to visit.

"You can meet Elias." Fabi fell back on the bed. "I *really* like him, Ben. He's kind. Smart, but not full of himself—"

"Not like me then." He grinned at her as he dressed.

"No, not like you." She rolled her eyes. "He is handsome though. His mother is Ethiopian. He's gorgeous. And so tall."

"You trying to make me jealous?"

"Is it even possible?"

Maybe. He couldn't decide yet. Fabi was an old friend, so it was nice to see her happy. That didn't mean he'd give this guy a free pass because she thought he was handsome. Ben was protective of the women in his life, especially the human ones.

He buttoned up the shirt. "So dinner with Angie and drinks after?"

"Yes. I called Ronan and Gabi too. They're going to

meet us. Gabi will want to sleep with you now that you have a beard. Ronan might too. Just warning you."

Ben laughed. "And yet, neither one is my type. It'll be good to see 'em both."

Ben and Fabi's group of friends in Rome mostly consisted of other young people who had—like them—grown up under vampire aegis in some way. Ronan's parents worked for Emil Conti, the immortal leader of Rome and most of Italy, while Gabi's family was involved with the vampires at the Vatican. Gabi and Ronan didn't offer information; Ben didn't ask.

When you grew up with vampires, you learned to be careful which questions you asked.

But it was easy to be with a group of people who understood where you were coming from. Darkness didn't hold the same allure when you grew up walking half your life in it. Their friends understood that.

"So why did you decide to come to Rome in June?" she asked as they walked toward the smell of meatballs. "Not that it's not nice to see you, but—"

"I'm visiting friends." He put his hand at the small of her back and ushered her into the courtyard where Angie was setting a small table for the three of them. "And I'm delivering some things for my uncle. And..." He sighed. "Still trying to figure out what I'm going to do, you know? Sometimes it's easier to think when I'm not in LA."

She touched his jaw in understanding. They'd spoken of post-university plans at Christmas.

"Any ideas yet?" Fabi asked.

"Maybe. Nothing definite. You?"

She shrugged. "I'm an attractive twenty-five-year-old Roman girl with degrees in archeology and art history. What do you think I'm going to do?"

"Tour guide?"

"Of course!" She smiled ruefully. "If I can build up a good private clientele, I can make a decent living. And I'll set my own schedule. I like that."

"I like the idea," Angela said as she placed a dish of olives on the table. "As long as she stays in the house and helps me here."

Ben raised his eyebrows. "Yeah? Like, permanently?"

"I'm thinking about it," Fabi said. "Zia Angela says she could use the help."

"I'm not getting any younger," Angie chided. "And Signor Giovanni will need another housekeeper when I must retire. It's a good job. And it will keep her busy when she's not leading tourists through the dust."

Ben smiled. He liked the idea. "I think you'd be great here. You already have your own room. Gio and B like you. Perfect solution."

Fabi rolled her eyes. "I haven't decided anything for certain. I like my apartment."

Ben looked around the lush courtyard with the palms and bougainvillea, the fountains providing trickling background music that echoed off the old walls surrounding them.

"Really?" he asked. "You like your apartment better than *this*?"

Angie leaned across the table. "Exactly. Listen to

Nino. You live in a palace here. Don't be stubborn. Come work for Signor Giovanni."

"Yeah," Ben said, popping an olive in his mouth. "Don't be stubborn, Fabi."

"You're one to talk, Ben Vecchio, he who likes to pretend he doesn't know exactly what he's going to do after university."

"I have no idea what you're talking about."

"Your uncle has been grooming you as a protégé for years, Ben. Are you really so clueless? He wants you to go into business with him."

Angie said, "Giovanni won't say anything; he doesn't want to pressure you."

Ben winced. It wasn't that Ben didn't know that Giovanni wanted him to work with him and Beatrice. Hell, he'd been unofficially working for his uncle since Giovanni had adopted him. But Ben was resisting it. Mostly because he just didn't know if he could spend the next seventy years sorting through dusty libraries, which —the rare adventure aside—was most of what his aunt and uncle did for clients.

"I'm thinking about it," he said. "Just... pass the wine, will you? I'm not going to decide tonight."

– ⊕ –

TENZIN watched the small group of young people from her perch by the statue. No one seemed to mind that she'd crawled up the embankment and sat next to the bronze chimera that had been mounted near the steps under the Ponte Cestio.

She caught Ben's expression and smiled. It was good to see him laughing. The past year at university had been stressful for him. He worked too hard to please his uncle. She knew part of Ben still considered any achievement a payment for the life of a boy rescued from the dirty slums of New York.

Ben didn't understand love yet. Not really.

But then, no one did when they were young. She leaned back against the cool stone and contemplated her latest plan to lure him in as a partner. She'd become bored in this modern world, and she needed something to do. Catching up on twentieth-century technology and mastering video games wasn't enough to keep her mind occupied.

No, she needed the rush of adrenaline again. She hadn't felt this restless since the days that she and Giovanni had been mercenaries.

Now *that* had kept her occupied.

But the world had changed. There was no longer any honor in living a warrior's life. Those who hired out their services as soldiers, even in the immortal world, were a different kind of animal than she and Giovanni had been, and she felt no kinship with them.

Ben turned and met her eyes in the low lights that reflected off the river.

Tenzin had a different kind of plan to occupy her time.

He stood and carefully wound his way through the outdoor tables and the small crowd watching a musician.

Then he stood under her, his chin just reaching the edge of the ledge where she was sitting.

"Did you think I wouldn't see you there?"

"I didn't think about it. I didn't want to disturb you and your friends."

He held out his hand. "Jump, don't float. Let the humans see gravity."

Tenzin jumped down and let her feet land hard. Such an awkward, heavy feeling. Yuck.

"Do you want me to leave you?" she asked.

"No, you're going to join us for a drink."

Tenzin halted. "No."

"Tiny, Fabi's the one who spotted you. Your cover as an inconspicuous statue has already been blown. You might as well come have a glass of wine."

Tenzin wasn't comfortable socializing outside her close circle of friends, and Ben knew it.

"Just try," Ben said, putting an arm around her shoulders. "All of them—except the tall Ethiopian guy—know about your kind anyway."

"Fine. One drink. And my Italian is rusty."

"We'll speak English then."

She made her way through the crowd of humans, automatically assessing threats and marking weapons. A surprisingly high number of them for a lazy summer evening, until she realized that two of the tables were surreptitious security for the young people at the table.

Interesting.

The guards immediately took note of Tenzin, and she felt Ben's arm tighten around her. He'd spotted them too.

Sometimes she was astonished by his perception. It was truly exceptional for one so young.

Fabia and Ben didn't warrant security from Giovanni, at least not under normal circumstances. She wondered whether socializing with Giovanni Vecchio's ward was considered something to be cautious about by other immortals. It could also be that there were current threats in Rome of which Tenzin hadn't been apprised. She'd have to give Giovanni a call later.

Until then, a far greater danger awaited her.

Small talk.

"Hey, guys!" Ben said. "This is Tenzin."

She saw the recognition immediately. Young people growing up under immortal aegis wouldn't have any idea what Tenzin looked like, but almost everyone in their world—human or vampire—knew her name.

The ancient one.

Daughter of Penglai.

Commander of the Altan Wind.

Assassin.

Spy.

Tenzin had been a legend before most of the Western immortals took their first breath.

Ben pressed a hand to her back and eased her into a chair he pulled next to his.

Only Ben, his friend Fabi, and her clueless boyfriend were at ease.

"Tenzin, it's so good to see you," Fabi said. "How long are you in town?"

Tenzin smiled. Fabi was Angela's niece. A smart, humorous girl. Ben was at ease with her, so Tenzin could be too.

"I'm here for a time," she said vaguely. "I have some business in the south, then I'll probably head north to visit some property."

She had a house in Venice. It was one of her favorites. Had she ever told Giovanni about it? She couldn't remember. She'd show Ben.

Ben said, "You know Ronan and Gabi, I think. And this is Elias, since Fabi is being rude—"

"*Zitto*!" Fabi laughed. "Sorry, I forgot. I feel like Tenzin must know everyone."

The young man leaned forward and held out a hand. "It's a pleasure to meet you. You're an American friend of Ben's?"

Tenzin stared at the hand for a moment before she held hers out, touching the young human's fingers only briefly so he didn't notice the unnatural chill of her skin.

"I am," she murmured, careful to keep her lips closed and her fangs covered. "It's a pleasure to make your acquaintance."

Ben seemed at ease with the young man. His earlier stiffness had eased the more he talked with Fabia's new friend. If Ben approved of the young man, Tenzin would give him the benefit of the doubt.

Ben quickly led the conversation into a discussion of a current film that had just premiered in Rome. Tenzin sipped the wine he poured for her and smiled, but she avoided speaking. Elias didn't know about immortals, and it was too difficult to conceal her nature from ignorant humans.

Ronan and Gabi's tension eased after a few moments, and soon the young people were drinking, joking, and laughing like the old friends they were. Tenzin, however, watched Ben.

Did he have friends like this in Los Angeles? He must have, but she didn't know them. When she was in LA, she didn't socialize except with Giovanni and his family. It was fascinating to see Ben in his element with the other humans his age.

He was a natural leader. He steered the conversation without effort, probably not realizing the others followed his lead. He was the kind of man other males would follow, not out of fear but because he made them feel a part of something greater. More important.

And with the females... Tenzin couldn't stop the smile.

Every girl Ben met fell half in love with him whether she wanted to or not. He was handsome, yes, but even more, she knew he truly enjoyed women and all their facets.

He caught her smiling at him.

"What?" he whispered.

Tenzin switched to Mandarin. "It was good for you to come here. You will see things more clearly."

"What things?"

She didn't answer him but leaned close and brushed a cool kiss over his bearded cheek. "I told you the beard was a good look for you. All the girls in the restaurant want to have sex with you."

He shook his head. "Seriously, Tiny—"

"I'm going to go. You're going to see Zeno tomorrow night?"

He nodded.

"I'll find you. Good night, my Benjamin."

"Night."

She waved to the others but slipped away without another word. She stepped lightly through the crowd, marking the humans and few vampires who were patronizing the festival that night. She kept her head down, and within moments, she was past the lights of the riverbank. Past the clatter of humanity.

Tenzin melted into the comforting shadows and disappeared.

Chapter Two

THE VATICAN LIBRARY MIGHT HAVE been the most famed, mysterious library in the Western world, but Ben still thought it smelled like most libraries everywhere. Dust. Mold. A stale smell he associated with institutional cleaners. He leaned back at the table in Zeno Ferrera's workroom and kicked his feet—newly shod in the best Italian leather thanks to his shopping trip with Fabi—on the table.

Zeno knocked them down. "Don't make me beat you."

The surly immortal had worked for his uncle over a year now, but he still held his connections with the church. Zeno had been a priest, and he was relatively young for an immortal, though he had been middle-aged when he'd been turned. He was just over one hundred years or something like that. Ben knew better than to ask.

"Grumpy old man," Ben muttered. "And after I brought you presents too."

Zeno waved a dismissive hand. "The journal will get at least one of our more... persistent clients off my back. He showed up at the library unannounced last week and surprised Fina. She wasn't pleased."

"I'm surprised he's still alive."

"Yes." Zeno drew out the word. "I think he is too."

The grumpy vampire had married the human librarian who ran Giovanni's library in Perugia, and he was rabidly possessive of both the woman and her young son.

"Fina and Enzo coming to Rome?"

"And swelter in this heat?" Zeno asked. "It's cooler at home. And Enzo's still finishing his school term. I think we'll take a holiday to the mountains if the weather doesn't let up. She's been asking for one, and the Naples theft..." Zeno shook his head and muttered under his breath. "It's been driving both of us crazy."

"Was it that bad?" Ben had a hard time understanding his family's obsession with books.

It wasn't that Ben didn't love books. He'd been a voracious reader since before he'd met Giovanni. Books were one of the few cheap and available escapes he'd had as a child. Alcohol made his mother cry. Drugs were expensive and dangerous.

But stories...

He'd split any time he could get away from his mother between the public library and the Metropolitan museum. But he couldn't understand the overriding desire to preserve medieval tax records or Renaissance-era farming manuals like they were made of precious metal.

"We don't know how big the Naples theft was," Zeno said. "That's part of the problem. And it wasn't just books."

"What does that mean?"

Zeno raised an eyebrow. "Valuables, my friend. Artifacts."

Okay, now his interest was piqued. Ben leaned forward. "I didn't hear Gio mention any artifacts. What's missing?"

"We don't know unless a client tells us. And your uncle doesn't deal in antiquities. Only books."

Ben's excitement fled. Bummer. Artifacts would have been interesting.

"A large portion of the library was uncatalogued," Zeno continued, paging through Giovanni's notes. "Partly because it's so old, and partly because many immortals used it like their own personal storage unit."

"That seems... unusual."

Zeno shrugged. "It's Naples. They're crazy down there."

Ben laughed.

"I can say that," Zeno said, "because I was born there. It's the truth." He tapped his temple. "Everyone from Naples... We're a little off, yes? We like it that way. Keeps life interesting."

"Makes me think I should be hanging out in Naples more."

"No, you shouldn't," Zeno said, shutting him down. "Maybe in another hundred years when there's a different vampire in power."

Ben pursed his lips. "So... when I'm dead."

Zeno frowned. "Why?"

"What?"

"I always assumed Giovanni would sire you. Why

wouldn't he? You're his son."

"I'm his nephew."

"So?"

"And I don't want to be a vampire."

Zeno shook his head. "You're a fool."

"No," he said. "I'm just not a romantic."

Zeno threw his head back and laughed. "And what is romantic about this life? Drinking blood? Hiding from the sun?" Then his amusement fell. "Watching old friends die?"

"Exactly. Do you wonder why I don't want it?"

"Yes." The old vampire narrowed his eyes. "Because I see the same thing in you that I could see in myself at your age. You're greedy."

It pricked Ben a little. Made him feel like he was asking for more than his share. He sat a little straighter. "There's nothing wrong with wanting—"

"Don't be offended. I understand it," Zeno said. "I wanted many things at your age. Money. Good music. Cheerful friends." Zeno grinned. "Many, many women."

Ben shrugged carelessly.

"I see much of myself in you, Ben. The same... ambition that drove me. The same greed."

"I don't see ambition as greed."

"I'm not talking about money," Zeno said. "Not talking about anything that... unimportant. I scraped coins growing up. I know just how good it feels to accumulate wealth. But that's not the kind of greed I'm thinking of. You're greedy for time, Ben Vecchio."

Ben stayed silent.

"Time," Zeno said, "is the true treasure of this life. And who is more greedy for time than those of us clinging to the dark?"

"You told me once you didn't want to become a vampire," Ben said quietly.

"I didn't!" Zeno said, sorting papers into a pile that he carefully placed in a grey document box. "I *didn't* want to be a vampire. But that didn't mean my sire was an idiot." Zeno winced. "Unfortunate that I killed him before I knew that wasn't strictly allowed. But he knew I'd come to terms with it."

"Why?"

"Because I was a thief!" Zeno said with a grin. "And a gambler. And because in the end, my sire helped me pull off the greatest heist of my life. *I stole time.*"

– ⊕ –

BEN was helping Zeno sort letters two hours later when a timid priest knocked at the door and peeked in.

"Brother Zeno?"

"Why do you bother me?" Zeno roared. "Can you not see that I am working?"

The priest flinched. "There is a... person here to see you and your guest."

"Who?" Zeno frowned. "I'm not expecting anyone."

"She was most insistent."

"Is it my wife?"

"No," the priest said quickly. "Though I have not met the *signora*, I am sure—"

The young man broke off when surprised shouts echoed down the hallway. Tenzin flew over the young priest's head, shoving him down and landing in front of Zeno with a smile.

"Oh," Zeno said. "It's you. I wasn't expecting you."

"Nobody expects me!" she said.

"Or the Spanish Inquisition," Ben muttered.

"What?"

Ben cleared his throat. "Nothing, Tiny. Why are you here?"

She flew over and sat in the center of the worktable as the young priest abandoned the room with relief.

"I was bored. And I wanted to talk to Zeno about Naples."

Ben leaned against the table. "Oh, are we being forthcoming this time?"

She shrugged. "There's not so much mystery. There is a vampire there who wants me to find some old coins for him. I want you to help."

Zeno's eyes shot up. "Who?"

"Who what?"

"Who wants you to find the coins?"

"Alfonso." Tenzin scooted over and swung her leg over the edge of the table, shoving Ben's carefully organized papers to the side. "Who else?"

Zeno's eyes darted between Tenzin and Ben. "And you intend to take Giovanni's son with you?"

"Yes," Tenzin said.

"I'm not Gio's son. And you haven't actually asked me to go with you," Ben said, crossing his arms. "I'm not going unless you tell me the details. And that includes any cross-Atlantic steamer trips I might be unknowingly booked on."

Zeno started laughing.

Tenzin flew behind Ben and perched on his back, hanging her arms over his shoulders. "Don't be mad. Didn't you get an excellent grade in Conversational Mandarin the next semester?"

"Not the point."

Zeno was still laughing. "I want to hear that story."

"It's really not that funny."

Tenzin said, "It really is."

"Tiny, if you want me—"

"I'll give you all the details. I already told you about the Sicilian coins, didn't I?"

"Mentioning a type of coin isn't a story. That's a detail. Is this another one of your caches? Is this someone who hired you? What will I be doing? Will any weapons be involved?"

"Such a pacifist." She sighed. "So boring."

How did she piss him off *so* quickly?

He untangled her arms from around his neck and shoved her away. "Fine. If I'm so boring, then you can—"

"Ask me your questions," Zeno barked. "Then take your lovers' quarrel somewhere else. I don't want to listen to it."

"He's not my lover," Tenzin said. "He's my... life coach."

Ben and Zeno both stared at her.

"What?" she said. "You don't like it when I call you

my human, so I've been thinking of other things I can call you instead of that."

Ben could feel the headache starting in his temples. "Do you even know what a life coach is?"

She threw up her arms. "Does anyone really know what a life coach is? I'm living in Los Angeles. They'll just think I've gone crazy."

"—*er*," Ben said. "Crazi*er*. And don't call me your life coach."

Zeno asked, "So what are you?"

"I'm..." Ben sighed. "I don't know. Impatient to hear the rest of this."

"Fine." Tenzin hopped off his back and onto the table. "I wanted to ask Zeno some questions anyway."

"Ask me what?"

"About Alfonso," she said. "He's the one who wants me to find his lost Sicilian tarì."

"Tarì," Zeno said. "Medieval tarì?"

Tenzin nodded. "These were minted during the twelfth century by Roger the Second."

"I don't think of Roger as a very Italian name," Ben said.

"He wasn't. He was Norman." Zeno stepped forward. "Truly? Twelfth-century tarì?"

"Alfonso had a very large chest of them. Rare, but I think they have sentimental value of some kind."

Zeno asked, "Was this chest in the library in Naples?"

"The big heist?" Tenzin grinned. "No, I don't think so, but I don't know the details. I just know Alfonso used to have them, and now he doesn't. And he wants me to find them."

Ben was suspicious. "Why you?"

"Because I'm good at finding things." She paused. "And I might have let it slip in some circles that I'd heard rumors about a hoard of medieval gold coins."

Ben's suspicions grew. "And had you? Heard rumors?"

She cocked her head to the side. "Not... precisely."

"It figures," Ben said, gathering up his messenger bag. "Zeno, do you have any weapons I can use? I have a feeling this is going to be one of *those* vacations."

"I didn't invite you on vacation!" she yelled. "I told you this was a working holiday."

"Yes," Zeno interrupted. "Working in *Naples*. Does Giovanni know?"

"No," she said. "Does he need to?"

"Well yes, because *Alfonso is crazy*," Zeno said. "And you're taking his son there."

"Not his son!"

"Alfonso hired me," Tenzin said. "And I've met him before... I think. I hardly think he's going to hurt Ben or me unless we try to double-cross him."

"Well yes," Zeno said. "It's entirely possible that you will get there and he will decide you have offended him in some inexplicable way and he'll kill you. Because he's *mad*. They call him the Mad Spaniard."

Ben turned to Zeno. "Like... regularly? That's his regular nickname? The Mad Spaniard?"

Why, why, *why* did she think this was a good idea?

"Not all the time," Zeno said.

Tenzin added, "Sometimes they call him the Mad Duke."

"So much better!" Ben threw up his hands and started pacing.

"But I don't know if he was really a duke or not." Tenzin shrugged. "It might just be one of those rumors. And Zeno, Alfonso could certainly *try* to hurt Ben or me," Tenzin said through a wicked smile. "That might be entertaining."

"Not from my perspective," Ben said.

"What do you want to know?" Zeno asked.

"What is his political situation right now?"

"Tenuous," Zeno answered. "But it is always so. His longest-serving advisor is a vampire named Filomena. She's powerful but doesn't seem to want the spotlight. Known to be vicious. You'd like her, I think."

"Because she's vicious?" Ben asked.

Zeno smiled. "Because she's straightforward. Filomena is probably the only reason Alfonso has stayed in power this long. She tempers him. The *napoletana* court is small, paranoid, and insular. Many of them came to Naples before Bonaparte. They don't truly consider themselves Italian, and they don't recognize Rome."

Ben asked, "And Emil Conti lets them get away with that?"

Zeno shrugged. "Naples is not his concern at present, though it would be better if the library theft had not happened. Now people are paying attention to it. Now some of his own people have lost possessions, which is why he's been putting pressure on Giovanni and Beatrice to take on Roman clients. Mostly Conti would like to pretend that Naples does not exist. Alfonso *does* pretend that Rome does not exist. As long as the status quo is maintained, everyone is happy."

Tenzin's head fell back. "The status quo is boring."

"And safe." Ben patted her head. "Remember that part."

"Fine," she said. "So we avoid pissing Alfonso off, keep Filomena in sight if things look like they're going... sideways, find his gold, and get out of there."

"Alfonso is known to be greedy," Zeno said. "If he wants you to find his gold, make sure you don't keep any souvenirs."

Tenzin's eyes went big and round. "Would I do that?"

"Yes," Ben said. Then to Zeno, "Yes, she would. Which is usually why Gio doesn't mind if I tag along on these kinds of things. I'll keep her out of trouble."

Tenzin's impish smile spread.

"Oh yes," Zeno said. "Obviously."

– ⊕ –

THE train to Naples was only an hour. He dozed in the sun, then grabbed another taxi from the station to Piazza Bellini, just south of the Archeological Museum. It was late afternoon, and the black stone streets of Naples were sweltering. He ducked in from the piazza and entered the quiet, flower-filled courtyard with a fountain at one end. The building was old. The furnishings were modern.

"*Buongiorno,*" the hostess at the front desk said when he opened the door.

Ahhhhh.

A rush of cool air. He stood for a moment, eyes closed, reveling in the air-conditioning.

"*Signore?*"

"Hey," he finally said in English. "I have a reservation under Benjamin Rios."

She smiled and answered in English. "Your passport, please?"

He pulled out a passport and handed it to her. Ben wasn't sure why he was using the fake passport Gavin had helped him procure last year in New York. He hated using his father's last name, but it made the most sense. He'd answered to Benjamin Rios for nearly twelve years, after all. Now the name only existed as a useful shadow.

The girl checked him in and handed him the key and a map directing him to his room. It was a small hotel, but it was perfectly located and had terrace rooms, which was necessary when he was traveling with Tenzin.

The hallway was sweltering, but the room was cool. Ben unlocked the french doors leading out to the terrace, closed the drapes, and decided to take a nap.

And woke to Tenzin on the bed beside him.

"This is starting to become a habit when we travel, Tiny."

"You're not naked this time. I checked."

He kept his eyes closed and shook his head. She'd

checked. Of course she had.

"This bed isn't as comfortable as your bed in Rome," she complained.

"Yeah..." He yawned and rolled toward her. "I didn't pick it because of the beds. I picked it because it has a private terrace. That way you can come and go as you please. This place seems to be pretty quiet, so I think you'll be okay."

"Awww." She patted his cheek. "You're such a thoughtful life coach."

"Please don't call me your life coach. That would make me feel responsible for any bodies you leave in your wake."

She laughed.

"Are we meeting Alfonso tonight?" he asked.

"Yes. Despite my somewhat flippant attitude with Zeno, I don't want to linger in the city too long. I want to meet Alfonso, make the deal, and fly out of here. We have three weeks, and that should be just enough time if we're smart."

"Want to fill me in?" he asked. "Now that Zeno's not here to tattle to Gio?"

"I will." She frowned. "But not yet. I want to get your impressions of Alfonso's court without any background information. Is that fair to you?"

He shifted on the bed. "I get it. His chief advisor—"

"Filomena."

"Yeah, Filomena. Are we meeting her tonight too?"

Tenzin nodded. "She's the one meeting us at Piazza del Gesù Nuovo at ten o'clock tonight."

"Do we have time to get dinner?"

"Always hungry. Always, always hungry."

– ⊕ –

SHE watched him as he chatted with an artist and munched on the hot *sciurilli* he'd picked up from a street vendor. She'd sampled a few of the delicately fried zucchini blossoms before she handed them over to Benjamin to demolish.

A group of rowdy street children ran into the square, shouting and laughing. Tenzin watched them spot Ben, his fashionable new clothes and Roman accent making him what the boys thought would be an easy target.

She watched the children slyly kick the ball closer and closer until the artist was yelling at one boy for disturbing his display and one of the others bumped into Ben, the child laughing and apologizing as he dipped into Ben's pocket...

And came out squealing. Ben clapped a hand over the boy's mouth and grabbed him by the back of the neck, dropping the fried snacks he'd been eating as the artist rushed to gather the prints that had gone flying with the soccer ball. Ben crouched down next to the boy, pinching his small hand in his own and speaking fiercely as the boy's cheeks turned bright red.

A few seconds later, the boy was running after his compatriots, who had abandoned him, a five-Euro note clutched in his hand, while Ben helped the artist pick up the last of his prints and a stray dog finished off the *sciurilli* that had fallen.

Ben walked over to a nearby street fountain and washed his hands before he shook them off and walked back to Tenzin.

"Pizza?"

She smiled and shook her head. "What did you tell him?"

"To be more careful choosing his marks."

"You didn't try to warn him away from a life of crime?"

Ben looked down the side street where the boy had disappeared. "I did a lot worse when I was hungry." He nodded toward a pizzeria on the corner. "Come on. I'll buy you a slice. Hopefully this Filomena won't be late."

Chapter Three

BEN SPOTTED THE VAMPIRE ENTERING Piazza del Gesù Nuovo a few minutes before ten. She was tall, especially for an immortal. With notable exceptions like his uncle, humans turned before the last century tended to be shorter than average. Tenzin was a perfect example. She was tiny, though she protested that she'd been quite tall for her time.

This vampire was wearing high-heeled boots and leggings with a long, sleeveless tunic that showed off lightly muscled arms. Caramel-brown hair flowed down her back, and her skin was pale with a slight pink flush that told Ben she'd fed earlier in the evening. No one turned to look at her as she crossed the square, even though she was wearing sunglasses at night, which made Ben think she was a familiar sight in the neighborhood. Though she looked young, he knew she wasn't.

She was also drop-dead gorgeous.

Ben knew the vampire had spotted Tenzin, who was perched on the graffiti-covered base of the monument in the center of the piazza, but Ben hung back, wanting to observe Alfonso's lieutenant for a few more moments before he drew her attention.

She was confident. He couldn't see any weapons on her, but she approached Tenzin with what could almost be called a swagger.

It was unusual in the immortal world. Though humans rarely noticed Tenzin which she loved—something about her made most immortals pause. Beatrice had told him once that Tenzin's amnis "smelled ancient," whatever that meant. If he'd been able to detect it like vampires did, he might have been intimidated.

But he was human, so she was just Tenzin.

"You are Tenzin," the vampire said when she reached the center of the square.

"Yes."

Tenzin didn't rise to her feet. Just looked up at the other vampire, squinting a little, her chin resting in her palm.

The street boys who'd been hanging around sank back into the crowds on the edge of the square, leaving the vampires alone, save for Ben, whom Filomena finally noticed. She looked him up and down with an appraising eye.

"I am Filomena. Who is the human?"

"This is Ben, my yoga instructor." Tenzin didn't bat an eye, so Ben didn't either. He just started plotting how on earth he was going to pay her back for that one. Was yoga instructor better or worse than life coach?

To Filomena's credit, she didn't blink. "Will he be accompanying you?"

"Yes."

"Fine." Filomena jerked her head. "Come. Alfonso is waiting."

Tenzin rose and followed Filomena, who led them

43

toward the odd stone building that dominated the square. Covered in pyramid-faced stones, the church of Gesù Nuovo was deserted, visiting hours long past. No matter. Filomena knocked at the wooden door and stood back until it swung open. She passed something to the priest at the door and ducked inside.

Tenzin and Ben followed her, neither meeting the eyes of the human in black robes who closed the door behind them. The heavy thunk echoed in the empty church. It was dark, except for a few candles lit in each chapel.

Baroque art assaulted Ben's eyes. Paintings, statues, and intricate altar pieces. "More" seemed to be the overriding design scheme. Filomena led them down a hallway covered with brass plaques and medals shaped like various body parts. Hearts and lungs. Legs, heads, and hands. The disembodied parts plastered the walls of the narrow hallway, lending a surprisingly morbid air to the holy place.

"For healing," Filomena said when she caught him looking. "Pilgrims come and pray here. They hang medals to ask for healing."

Ben smiled, delighted in the excess. "Does it work?"

Filomena blinked. "Of course not. It's superstition. Humans are very gullible."

He saw the edge of Tenzin's smile when he passed her.

The hallway led to a back room with a hidden door behind a tapestry. Then another hallway and another door. Ben could feel the cool damp growing the farther they traveled. At his side, he felt Tenzin's tension increase.

"Where are you leading us?" she asked.

"Alfonso keeps court under the city," Filomena explained. "He prefers the seclusion."

Only Ben caught the minute falter in Tenzin's step.

"That's unusual, isn't it?" Ben asked, stepping quickly into her silence. "I was told Alfonso was a water vampire."

"He is."

No other explanation came, nor did he expect one. Filomena pressed on, turning corner after corner until Ben was completely baffled. It was a maze, designed to confuse those not familiar with it. Plaster hallways gradually gave way to stone passages. Then Filomena stopped at a wooden door and pulled out an old iron key.

She said nothing as she unlocked the door and swung it open, the damp musk of earth blasting them as an even darker passageway gaped below. Filomena didn't wait for them to enter. She handed Ben a flashlight from a shelf set into the wall and continued down the wooden stairs leading below the surface.

Ben watched Tenzin. Her tension had been steadily growing the farther they traveled. Now her face was a complete mask. Dead eyes. Face devoid of expression. He'd never seen her look less human.

"Tiny?" he murmured.

"Go. I don't need the light."

Something was very wrong.

"Do you want me to—"

45

"Walk, Benjamin."

She shoved him toward the stairs and followed him, but Ben grabbed hold of one of her cold hands and held it, disturbed beyond reason by the look in her eyes. He walked down the damp, earthen passage leading under the streets of Naples.

Tenzin wasn't claustrophobic. The mere idea of it was ridiculous. She'd comfortably traveled across much of China in a smuggler's hatch once. What the hell was going on?

He refused to let go of her hand, even when she tried to tug it away. Finally she seemed to give up and let Ben hold it as they walked down the stairs, following Filomena into the darkness. The vampire slowed down to allow for the clumsy human to stumble along. The passageway was smooth, but the dirt floor was uneven.

"How do you walk in those heels?" he asked Filomena.

A low laugh. "Natural grace and centuries of practice."

Ben smiled.

He followed her for what felt like an eternity before the earthen passageway gave way to stone again, and he felt the tension begin to ease from Tenzin's fingers. Another turn and they entered an arched chamber nearly the size of a gymnasium.

"What is this?" he asked Filomena.

"One of the catacombs," she said. "Naples has many tunnels. Alfonso has used this system for years. The humans don't come here."

Ben ran his fingers along one wall. "This construction looks Roman."

"It is."

He couldn't help but smile. It was like walking through a ruin, only perfectly preserved from sun and weather. Arches soared over his head along with a series of walkways leading from the second story into other tunnels. There were no electric lights, but torches lit the hall and the air was fresh, so he knew there had to be ample ventilation. He could hear water flowing somewhere. It must have been what drew Alfonso to this place.

Hidden from the sun. No electricity. Secret passages. Underground water.

"It's brilliant," he said under his breath.

Tenzin, seemingly fully recovered from whatever had plagued her in the earthen tunnel, nodded in agreement.

"A most comfortable court," she said. "I am impressed, Filomena."

"On behalf of my lord, I thank you," Filomena said, nodding respectfully toward Tenzin. "The immortals of Naples are very proud of our city."

"As you should be."

– ⊕ –

TENZIN hated being underground. Absolutely hated it. She couldn't remember the last time she'd frozen as she had on the stairs.

It wasn't the close passageway. It wasn't even the

47

knowledge that they were going beneath the earth. It was damp air. The closed passage. The taste of the earth and rot in the air surrounding her.

The taste of earth in her mouth...

She'd heard ancient laughter in the back of her mind, and the wary creature in her emerged. The gut-deep urge for blood took root, and she concentrated on the pounding of the young one's pulse.

Th-thunk. Th-thunk. Th-thunk.

She followed it in her mind, pacing his steps. Following his blood. But something stopped the creep of amnis before it reached his skin. Some instinct whispered to the feral creature, coaxing it to calm.

They walked into a tunnel built of rock, and the smell of earth receded. The pressing eased on her mind.

There was nothing but the taste of earth that could cause that old reaction to emerge. Tenzin found she was still holding Ben's hand. It showed weakness, but she did not let go until they entered a larger hallway clad in dressed stone, when the rotting earth had receded and her sanity had returned.

Mostly.

Filomena led them under the Roman arches of subterranean Naples and toward her master, who was sitting on a raised dais playing king of all he surveyed.

Tenzin disliked him immediately.

He wasn't a handsome vampire. His face was pockmarked and sagging. His skin had once been olive, but now it leaned toward sallow. A high forehead, arched nose, and haughty gaze led her to believe he was, as he claimed, Spanish royalty of some kind.

Filomena stopped at the edge of the dais and gave Alfonso a short bow.

"Alfonso," she began in English, "I introduce Tenzin, daughter of Zhang Guolao. Sired of air. Mated to water..."

Oh, so he was one of *those* immortals. Tenzin tried not to sigh as Filomena continued.

"...Scourge of the Naiman Khanlig. Commander of the Altan Wind. Protector of Penglai Island. Patron goddess of the Holy Mountain..."

Goddess of anything holy, let it end.

"...protector and scribe of New Spain. Friend of Don Ernesto Alvarez of Los Angeles." Filomena paused. "And... Ben, her yoga instructor."

Ben leaned over and whispered, "You have so many more titles than I realized."

"You have no idea."

"I need to be called 'The Scourge' of something. Just put that in the back of your mind to think about later."

"Maybe the Scourge of the Refrigerator," she muttered. "That would be accurate."

Ben must have realized that a dozen or so vampires were staring at the two of them because he straightened, cleared his throat, and whispered, "Sorry." He stepped just behind Tenzin and to the left, instinctively covering her weaker side.

Tenzin, not wanting to piss off the vampire who would be paying her lots and lots of money if everything went according to plan, inclined her head and said,

"Thank you for your generous welcome, Alfonso."

"Welcome to Naples," Alfonso grunted. "It is one of the few civilized places left on the peninsula."

"I have found it remarkably civilized," Tenzin said. "And very rich. In history. And... culture."

And gold, but Alfonso would probably find that crass. There were a few artifacts in the archeological museum that Tenzin was considering liberating from their cases. Some things just shouldn't be forced behind glass.

"As you are here, I assume you received my communication regarding the gold."

"I did."

"The Norman tarì are mine." Alfonso's eyes burned. "Whatever rumors you might have heard, any knowledge of them should be given to me. Withholding information that might lead to their return would be very unwise."

"I have long welcomed," Tenzin said quietly, "the opportunity to assist my... friends in the retrieval of valuable possessions, should those possessions be lost or misplaced." She raised her voice enough for the other immortals to hear it. "But be careful, son of Kato. I do not respond well to bullying."

– ⊕ –

GOOD Lord, some vampires were stupid, no matter how long they lived. Ben repressed the urge shake his head. Who heard the litany of titles Tenzin carried—*the Scourge of the Naiman Khanlig?* What was *that* about?

—and then proceeded to threaten the Scourge?

Tenzin was quietly schooling Alfonso, so Ben made mental notes about the Neapolitan court. Lucky for him, most of these vampires were traditional and completely ignored the human in their midst.

Filomena, he noted, did not. In fact, she was watching him more than she was Tenzin. And the slight curve at the corner of her gorgeous mouth told him she'd like to get to know Tenzin's "yoga instructor" a little more.

Ben returned her smile with a wink.

Filomena's eyebrows rose, but she did not look displeased.

Tenzin was speaking in a lower voice to Alfonso. The two leaned together, engaged in a private conversation. Alfonso scowled, but Ben didn't get the impression he was displeased.

Filomena sidled up to him. "He always looks like that."

"How? Pissed?"

Filomena clearly didn't understand the American slang.

Ben quickly said, "Sorry. I mean angry."

"Ah." She nodded. "Yes, Alfonso nearly always looks angry. And he often is. But I believe he and your pupil are merely negotiating some arrangement regarding the coins she's heard rumors of."

Ben was confused. "My pupil?"

Filomena cocked her head. "You are her yoga instructor, are you not? I admit, I did not know that a warrior such as Tenzin was so spiritually inclined, but I find it inspiring that she is so. She must be very devout to bring you with her, even across oceans."

"Right." Ben tried to look very solemn. "Well, I'm kind of her... spiritual advisor too."

"Of course."

"So you find Tenzin inspiring, huh?"

She blinked. "She is one of the most ancient of our race. A woman of tremendous power and influence."

"And you?"

"I'm young." Her mouth curled into a smile. "But not so young as you."

Filomena's eyes traveled across his chest and up his neck while she let the edge of her fangs peek from her bottom lip.

It was the vampire version of a proposition, and Ben's body responded with enthusiasm.

"Will you be remaining in Naples?" she asked.

I will be now.

Ben forced himself to remember his role. "That depends on Tenzin, of course."

Filomena glanced at Tenzin and Alfonso, who were still locked in conversation. "And you do not belong to her?"

Hell no.

He put his solemn face back on. "I hope you understand that I take my spiritual commitments very seriously. I could never involve myself with someone under my instruction."

Her fangs dropped lower. "I have heard that those

who practice the eastern arts exhibit great flexibility and vigor."

Ben didn't even hear Tenzin approach until she interrupted.

"Yes," she said. "Ben is very vigorous. Shall we go?"

He blinked. "What? I... Yes. I mean, if you're done with your conversation with Alfonso. Then yes."

She looked amused. "I am. Filomena, your master said you could see us out. The front door this time, please."

Filomena glanced over Ben's shoulder and nodded at whoever was behind him. Ben was assuming Alfonso, but he didn't turn to look. Yoga instructors wouldn't be that curious, would they?

"Of course," she said, bowing a little as she motioned down a hall that was opposite the way they'd entered. "If you would follow me, my lady."

"No bowing, please. And call me Tenzin."

"I would be honored to do so."

Ben fell in step behind them as Filomena led them down another stone hallway and up a set of torchlit stairs. Within moments, they were exiting through the front of a dimly lit nightclub. Vampire and human patrons turned to glance at them, then quickly looked away.

Once they were out of the building, Ben looked around and realized they were close to his hotel on Piazza Bellini.

"Convenient," he muttered, looking around at the young people gathered across the street. Naples was alive

53

with humans and more than a few vampires. The sound of music and smell of tobacco filled the air. Ben saw paint-spattered artists and earnest students. Young men with slicked-back hair and girls in snug cocktail dresses.

Tenzin and Filomena were all business.

"I'll make contact when I locate the item," Tenzin said. "I would estimate three weeks, but I cannot say for certain. This will require a trip to Switzerland, you understand?"

"Of course," Filomena said. "We all understand the Swiss are... complicated. If he grows impatient, I will remind him of your words."

"Thank you."

"The thanks are mine." Filomena inclined her head. "The tarì are part of our treasury. You honor Naples with your assistance in this matter."

"I look forward to our continued cooperation," Tenzin said. "Ben, let's go."

He followed Tenzin, throwing Filomena one more smile over his shoulder. She returned it before he lost her in the crowd.

"Careful," Tenzin said.

"What?" He stopped looking for Filomena in the mass of people. "Careful what?"

"She's powerful. Ambitious too. And she's playing you."

Ben felt a bite of annoyance. "Listen, Tiny, I'm not a teenager—"

"If you think she doesn't know who you are, you're kidding yourself." Tenzin didn't look angry, only amused. "You don't actually think Alfonso's second believes I brought my yoga instructor to Naples, do you?"

Well, yeah, but he decided to play it off. "Good. That means I won't have to worry about bending into impossible shapes when we hook up."

Tenzin laughed. "'Hook up?' You act as if you'd be catching a fish on a line. Trust me, if anyone is the hunter in this situation, it is not you."

His cheeks burned. "This really isn't any of your business."

"On the contrary, it is certainly my business." Her face grew serious. "Human girls are one thing, but she's a three-hundred-year-old immortal. Have you had sex with a vampire before?"

He clenched his jaw in an effort to rein in his temper. It worked. Some. "That's none of your business either."

They walked into Piazza Bellini, the crowds of young people no less dense than they had been outside Alfonso's club. Tenzin walked Ben to the gates of his hotel and turned to face him.

"Sex is one thing, Benjamin. Don't let her bite you. We get possessive when we bite."

"Yeah, I know that."

She shrugged. "You'll do what you want. Just remember, don't sabotage this deal with your ignorant libido. Alfonso wants me to find his coins. You help me and you'll get twenty percent of the finder's fee, which is not insignificant."

Sex he didn't want to discuss, but money was always on the table. "Forty percent and I'm an altar boy until after we deliver the coins."

"Twenty-five. You may flirt, but you'd end up being an altar boy anyway. You're too smart to be her plaything."

"Who said I wouldn't be playing her? Thirty percent."

She cocked her head. "Done. I'm going to Switzerland tomorrow night. Go back to Rome and look busy. Help Zeno in the library. Maybe head to Perugia for a few days of research. I'll be in touch when I need you."

"Sounds like a plan, Tiny." Ben grinned. "Switzerland, huh? Don't forget to take a sweater."

Chapter Four

BEN SLEPT UNTIL NOON THE next day, then decided to wander around Naples and enjoy some of the street art the city was known for. More than one artist who'd gotten his or her start in graffiti had been signed by major agents in the past few years. It was fascinating to see the blend of styles. Art of any kind fascinated him, but street art, with its inherently fleeting nature, touched something in Ben's soul.

He stood at the mouth of an alley, staring down at a small white figure painted on the soot-black stone of an alleyway corner. The figure was holding a tiny sword high against a flying dragon. A red feather was perched in his cap.

The painting might have been there for months or hours. Who knew when city workers might come and paint over it? Another artist could come and wipe it away with something darker or brighter or coarser or more colorful. But the artist had taken the time, probably in the dead of night, to put her mark on that wall, hoping to touch a passerby. For the moment Ben looked at that tiny figure fighting off the dragon, Ben and the artist were in the same space.

Fleeting.

Like the painting.

Here today. Gone tomorrow.

He was the tiny hero with the feather in his cap, fighting things impossibly powerful. He was the painting on the wall. No grand masterpiece preserved and admired for eternity. His life would be a blink. A quick glance from the immortal pedestrians of history.

No wonder the little figure flew a red feather in his cap. No wonder his sword was held so high.

Tiny hope. Foolish courage.

Ben pulled out his phone and snapped a picture before he continued to walk down the Spaccanapoli, the narrow road splitting the heart of old Naples. He stopped for some gelato, then wandered some more. Bought a few trinkets in a shop. Watched a drummer when he finally arrived back in Piazza del Gesù Nuovo, the spiked facade of the church a reminder of his meeting the previous night.

Naples was... odd. Fiercely different from other Italian cities he knew. Gloriously excessive. He wished that Beatrice could visit. He knew she'd love it.

His phone buzzed in his pocket with a text message from Fabi.

T called the house. She said to make sure you go to the archeological museum before you meet your new girlfriend.

Ben texted back: *Ha-ha.*

??? Do I need to be jealous?

He shook his head. Leave it to Tenzin to try to cause trouble.

No, he texted back. *And don't you have a boyfriend?*

Never hurts to keep your options open. ;) I want details when you get back. Stay safe.

Always.

He pushed away from the wall where he'd been searching for shade and wandered back to the Piazza Bellini. The Museo Archeologico Nazionale di Napoli was only a few blocks from his hotel, and while he'd heard about the mosaic collection there—famous for its detailed relics from Pompeii—Ben had a feeling it was the coins and medals exhibit Tenzin wanted him to visit.

He wandered the grand halls, fanning himself with the museum map. The marble-clad museum was shady, but not particularly cool in the sweltering June heat. Still, he didn't hurry. It was better than fighting the crowds for shade outside.

The Pompeii mosaics really were everything the guidebooks said they'd be, but as he walked up the stairs to reach the gems room, he wondered what exactly Tenzin had wanted him to see. He'd seen more than his share of old currency. What was special about Naples?

The front desk had told him he was fortunate the rare coins exhibit was even open. As he entered, Ben was struck by the sheer number in the collection. Everything from Greek and Roman coins to medieval and modern. One room even contained dies from the old mint in Naples.

Norman *tarì*, Alfonso had said. Ben had looked up Norman *tarì* as soon as he'd arrived back at the hotel, but he didn't notice any in the collection. What he saw was a mix of metals in all different states and a whole lot of empty space as museum visitors took in the more dazzling treasures of the museum.

Norman *tarì*.

What was so special about these *tarì* that Alfonso would risk disrespecting Tenzin to get them back? Did Tenzin already know where they were? Is that why she'd gone to Switzerland?

Ben felt a twinge of jealousy that she'd abandoned him when he felt the bead of sweat roll down his temple. The beard and longer hair might have been a hit with the girls this summer, but he was tempted to find a barber and a razor that afternoon.

Instead, he went back to the hotel, drank two cold beers, and retreated to the shelter of his air-conditioned room for the remainder of the afternoon. When he emerged, the sun was down, the temperature had cooled, and a vampire wearing high-heeled boots was smoking a slim cigarette in the garden of his hotel.

Filomena smiled and blew out a thin stream of smoke. "You're awake."

Ben walked toward her. "So are you."

She shrugged one lightly muscled shoulder and nodded toward the piazza. "Join me for a drink, will you?"

Ben cocked his elbow out and Filomena rose, her boots putting her just a hair taller than Ben as they walked.

"So, Benjamin Vecchio"—Filomena leaned into his side—"what is the adopted nephew of a famed assassin doing in my city with his uncle's old partner?"

He really hated when Tenzin was right.

– ⊕ –

FILOMENA smiled at him in the candlelight, careful to conceal her fangs even when she laughed. "Was yoga instructor her idea or yours?"

"What do you think?"

"I hardly know. I only know Tenzin by reputation." She gave him another careless shrug. Such a human habit for an immortal. Did she do it out of true habit, or was it an affectation to put her prey at ease? Ben was drawn to her regardless.

They were sitting at a small table outside a quiet restaurant near the waterfront. The moon was high, reflecting off the Bay of Naples as shadowed ships bobbed in the distance. The waterfront was busy, but the restaurant she'd chosen was isolated down a small alley, which meant they didn't worry about being overheard.

Ben said, "I think everyone knows Tenzin's reputation."

"Yes." She sipped the red wine. A drop lingered on her lips before she licked it away. "Everyone does. And yet you were raised with her?"

Ben shook his head. "Not exactly. I only met Tenzin when I was sixteen."

"A child."

"Of a sort."

Ben couldn't remember ever feeling like a child. His earliest memory was of his parents in a fistfight, screaming at each other before his father threw his mother into a mirror. It was the sound of shattering glass and the taste of blood in his mouth that had stuck with him. His mother said a shard had sliced his lip. He still bore the tiny scar. And the rest of his "childhood" he simply tried to banish to the murky shadows of history.

"But what a childhood it must have been," she said. "To be raised among legends."

"What about your human life, huh?" He leaned forward, keen to take the attention off himself. "Do you remember... the Renaissance?"

Filomena laughed. "No."

It was a game. Vampires were notoriously secretive about their origins. To reveal their age meant revealing their power. But guessing and riddles were fair game.

"Italian unification?"

"Oh yes," Filomena said, her eyes flashing. "I remember that quite clearly."

"Napoleon."

"You're getting closer," she said, leaning a slim arm on the table, propping her chin in her palm. "You know I'm not going to tell you."

"But you are from Naples."

She smiled and he saw a hint of fang. "Define *Naples*."

Ben gave her a good-natured growl and threw up his hands. "I give up."

Filomena laughed. "You should know better, Benjamin Vecchio."

"Ben," he said. "Call me Ben."

Dark brown eyes appraised him. "And did your friends warn you away from me, Ben?"

"Of course." He leaned across the table until he heard her draw in his scent. He stared at her lips. "You may be a stunningly beautiful woman, but you're also a lethal immortal enforcer, second to one of the most dangerous vampire lords in Italy." He let the corner of his mouth turn up as he raised his eyes to hers. "And I am a mere yoga instructor. I'd be a fool to—"

The breath between them vanished when Filomena took his lips.

Hot. Ben closed his eyes and took her mouth as she had taken his, raising his hand to cup the nape of her neck. His fingers tangled in her thick, caramel-brown hair.

Filomena heated her skin until it matched the flush of his own. She tasted of wine and chocolate and the indefinable taste that was all her own. A medley of scent and flavor and sensation. Her eyelashes brushed his skin as he eased away from her mouth and trailed his lips along the arch of her cheekbone. He followed the fragrance of her hair and the perfumed skin beneath her ear.

Filomena let out a low, satisfied purr and dragged her nails down his neck.

The sharp bite of pain brought Ben up short.

Blood rushed back to his head as he trailed firm kisses back along her chin and up to her mouth again, luxuriating in her taste and the softness of her lips.

Her fangs were fully aroused.

Ben drew away, gently biting her lower lip before he smiled. "You taste delicious."

She blinked slowly. "And you are a cautious man."

He cupped the side of her neck, brushing his thumb over where her pulse would beat.

If she were human. Which she wasn't.

"Mmm," he said on a sigh. "Sadly, I have to be. After all, a foolish yoga instructor wouldn't last long in your world."

"*My* world?" Filomena raised an eyebrow, clearly still enjoying their flirtation. "Is it not your world as well?"

"That's an excellent question."

"One you're not going to answer."

"It's only our first bottle of wine, Filomena. We shouldn't reveal all our secrets at once."

"True."

She shrugged his hand off her neck, so Ben let it fall to the back of the chair in a proprietary gesture that seemed to please the vampire, judging by the smile teasing the corners of her mouth.

"You're bold."

"Am I?" *That's probably why I'm not dead already.*

Lucky for him, she only smiled and leaned against it, willing to play his game for the night. "You're also surprisingly good with your mouth. For a human."

"Thanks. I got kissing lessons from a three-hundred-year-old French courtesan when I was a teenager. I think it helped."

Filomena threw her head back and laughed loudly.

She even wiped a pink tear from the corner of her eye before she asked, "Is that true?"

"I'm not going to tell you."

She narrowed her eyes, trying to find his tell, but Ben smiled innocently.

"What?"

"It's a shame I cannot take you as a lover. I don't think either of us would regret it."

He let his eyes trace her mouth, the delectable cleavage she had bared for the evening, and the sweep of her long, muscled legs. "I think regret would be the last thing on my mind."

"This life is long."

He cocked his head. "Not for everyone."

"All the more reason to seize the night."

Ben shook his head and poured both of them more wine. "My friends were right. You are a dangerous woman."

$$- \oplus -$$

Rome, one week later

BEN kicked the ball back to Enzo, the boy whooping in delight as he ran after it in the courtyard. His mother, Serafina, watched from the bench near the fountain where she chatted quietly with Fabi as Ben and Enzo killed time before Zeno rose for the night.

The old vampire had finally convinced the quiet woman to marry him the Christmas before, though Fina had protested they should wait until her son was grown.

Ben was fairly sure his uncle would have a new immortal daughter once Enzo was an adult. Neither Fina nor Zeno had said anything, but Ben could see how devoted they were to each other. Plus they were both under Giovanni's aegis and invaluable members of his staff.

Fina had brought herself and Enzo to join Zeno in Rome as soon as the boy had finished his school exams for the year. Now the three were residing in Residenza di Spada with Ben and Angie.

Angie, of course, was delighted. Especially since that gave her three human appetites to cook for. Four if you counted Fabi, who ate dinner with them most nights.

"So Fina"—Ben interrupted the women's quiet conversation—"Zeno said you saw Tenzin at the library before she went north."

"Only briefly," Fina said. "I didn't speak to her. I think she only sheltered for the day before she flew away. Though she did take a fifteenth-century manuscript on metalsmithing. Well, the copy of it. I only have a digital scan because the original resides in—"

"Metalsmithing?" Ben frowned. *Metalsmithing?* But why would Tenzin need a manual on medieval metalsmithing if she already knew where Alfonso's cache...

Oh, Tenzin.

Shit.

He should have known.

"Ben," Fina continued, unaware his thoughts had wandered, "Zeno tells me that you and Tenzin are working for Alfonso in Naples. You are being careful, aren't you?"

"Of course." He kicked the ball back to Enzo just

before Angie called the boy inside the house to wash up. Ben strolled over to the edge of the fountain and perched on the corner. "What do you know about him?"

"Well"—Fina's prim voice made him smile—"it is rumored that he was part of the Bourbon court, but that is only a rumor. Like many things in Naples—well, and anything to do with immortals, if we're honest—rumors of corruption have followed him over the years. Giovanni is fairly certain he was behind the library theft."

Ben's eyebrows rose. According to what he'd been able guess from subtle questions to Filomena, much of the unrest in the Neapolitan court was *because* of the library theft. Many of the richest immortals in Naples had lost personal collections that were both valuable and highly confidential. Ben suspected it was one of the reasons Alfonso had risked calling Tenzin.

So if Alfonso himself was somehow behind the theft and hiding it from his own people...

"How sure are you?" Ben asked. "That the theft is because of Alfonso?"

"Fairly sure," Fina said. "Officially, the authorities arrested the former director of the library. He had very suspicious political connections, and some of the books that made it on the black market were traced back to him. But when I spoke to my friends familiar with the Girolamini Library, they were quite certain there was more to it than one man. There were portions of the collection that had never been catalogued. Parts they were unofficially told to ignore. That had been happening long before the former director came into his position."

"But why would Alfonso want to steal his own

people's papers and collections?"

Fabi, who'd been listening silently, said, "Power? Paranoia? Didn't your uncle say he was crazy?"

"Pretty sure Beatrice called him completely bonkers. Gio said something much more polite."

Fina smiled. "That sounds correct. Naples is... Well, it is different. I have always liked the city, but it is unique. Why wouldn't the immortal leader also be unique?"

"So if he was behind the theft...," Ben muttered. "Fina, how much of the theft have you tracked?"

"We're not tracking the whole theft. There's no way. Emil Conti asked, but Giovanni said he would only take on individual clients with specific items. And only books, of course. Those who lost antiquities have to rely on the human authorities. And most of them..." Fina shrugged. "Well, you know how secretive vampires are. They won't trust Italian police or Interpol."

Ben said, "So if I'm a vampire who lost... a coin collection, let's say"—Fabi shot eyes at him, but Ben ignored her—"you're saying there's no one like Gio who would track that down?"

Serafina shook her head. "Not that I'm aware of. No one with your uncle's reputation anyway. You could hire someone, but we're speaking about priceless artifacts, Benjamin. Many of which would only be legends or rumors to human sources."

"And"—a gruff voice broke into their quiet conversation as Zeno entered the courtyard—"we're paranoid bastards." He bent to press a hard kiss to Fina's mouth. "Are you well this night, my love?"

"Yes, Zeno."

"Good."

Ben cleared his throat loudly, and Fabi kicked him. He ignored her.

"So Zeno, why don't you think—?"

"How would one vampire trust another to retrieve an artifact for him or her without stealing it, eh?" Zeno sat next to Fina while she fussed with the collar of the shirt he'd obviously just tossed on. "Even if you did trust another vampire to find it, that immortal would be a target for the opportunistic ones. There are few vampires like your uncle who have trustworthy reputations *and* the ability to back up their word with power."

"But Gio won't look for anything but books."

"No, and I understand why. To do what we do"—he put an arm around his wife—"you must love it. You must have passion. Because often the work... It is dull, no? So many hours looking for one tiny clue that could lead you to another clue. Dead ends. Destroyed sources. Your uncle loves beautiful things, but he doesn't have the passion for art that he has for knowledge. It would be very convenient if we had someone who did."

Fabi kicked his shin again.

"Ow! Will you stop?"

Fabi just shook her head. "Nino, sometimes your head is full of rocks."

Chapter Five

Rio Terà dei Assassini, 3806 Venezia

"REALLY?" BEN LOOKED AT THE paper in his hand and the key that looked like it belonged somewhere in the seventeenth century. Then he looked at the seemingly incomprehensible address that had been left at the house in Rome the day before.

His low cursing must have attracted the attention of the young man setting out tables at the small osteria on the Rio Tera dei Assassini.

The young man smiled and called out to him, "Are you looking for something?"

"My friend's flat," Ben replied, tugging his messenger bag back up his shoulder and walking toward the waiter, valise in one hand and slip of paper in the other. "This address she gave me... I swear, I'll end up walking into the canal. I don't think it exists."

The young man frowned at the paper when Ben handed it to him. "I don't recognize this address either. Venice can be difficult. Sometimes the houses aren't marked. This one..." He craned his neck around the curve of the narrow street. "Yes, you're right. It should be on the corner next to the canal, but the number isn't correct."

"Great."

"Try to call her, yes?" The helpful young man smiled. "She must have written it down wrong."

"Yeah, probably."

"Or she doesn't really want to see you." The waiter laughed. "Women, no?"

"You have no idea with this one." Ben tapped his leg and felt the key in his pocket. "I think I'll go try the one on the end. You're right. She probably just wrote it down wrong. Thanks."

"Come back for a drink if you can't find her," the waiter said. "Nothing makes us forget them like wine."

Ben cracked a smile. "No such luck. This one is unforgettable."

He wandered down the street and waited, but it was dead quiet. The street was hardly wider than an alleyway back in LA. There were no shops and only a couple of quiet restaurants, neither of which looked like it catered to tourists. In the maze of Venice, this tiny street managed to be completely anonymous while only five minutes' walk from the madness of Piazza San Marco.

"Incredible," Ben said, leaning out over the canal where gondoliers pushed gawking tourists through the narrow canals. Some sang. Most chatted on their mobile phones.

Ah, Venice.

He had to admit, the note had been a surprise. What was Tenzin doing in Venice? What did this have to do with Alfonso's tarì? And where the hell did she expect him to go?

He was leaning on the end of the building, watching the gondolas push past when an old man shuffled out of the nearest door. It was a green maintenance door with electrical-shock warning signs screaming in yellow and various outlines blocked out. Apparently that doorway was not a good place to walk your dog.

The stocky old man turned to lock the green door and noticed Ben. He scowled, took a moment to look him up and down, then snorted while nodding.

"Okay," the man said, giving Ben a "hurry up" hand as he walked across to the opposite door. "What do I expect? Does she tell me anything? Of course she doesn't." He stopped and turned to Ben. "Do you have the key or not?"

"I think so?" Ben held up the key and the old man nodded and took it.

"Fine, fine."

The old man must have been Tenzin's caretaker. Or... something.

The old man kept grumbling. "'A friend soon,' she says. When is soon? Of course soon is three months later. Because I have nothing else to do but wait for her friends."

"Oh God." Ben had a depressing flash of insight that the old man could very well be a vision of his future. Fifty years from now, his youth gone, still managing to get pulled into Tenzin's schemes. "I need to rethink my life."

The old man opened a heavy wrought iron gate and raised a finger as he squinted at Ben. "Yes. You do. And don't forget to lock the gate on the way out. The code is written on the wall in the courtyard. Five hundred years old and she can't remember a gate code. She has to carve it into perfectly good plaster. Bah." He threw up his hands, let go of the gate just as Ben caught it, and walked away.

"Bye," Ben called. "Thanks."

The old man just threw up a tired hand and kept walking.

"Really, *really* need to rethink my life," Ben said under his breath as he hoisted his bag higher and walked into the entryway of...

One seriously cool house.

"Holy shit."

It was a "house" the same way Giovanni's house in Rome was a house. Just a Venetian version. There were rooms on either side of him, but a wide, open-air hallway led back to a lush green courtyard where an old marble fountain trickled and orange and lemon trees were espaliered along the walls, interspersed with raised beds of herbs and vegetables. Three stories up, arched windows opened over the courtyard, letting in whatever trickle of breeze the sweltering day allowed.

Past the courtyard, a wide entry hall floored in black-and-grey-checked marble led to a private dock with another elaborate wrought iron gate. White marble statues lined the entry, and Moroccan lanterns with brightly colored glass dripped from the ceiling. Ben could hear a gondolier whistling past the gate, but the man paid him no attention as he explored.

"This. Is. The. Coolest," he said. And a pretty

73

brilliant setup for an air vampire. He kept in the shadows of the entry hall and realized that, except for the courtyard, the whole first floor was light safe. No direct sunlight could get in with the high walls and soaring buildings across the canal. At night the private, open-air courtyard would give Tenzin access to the rooftops of Venice while the canal, though not ideal for an air vampire, provided another exit route.

He wandered up a half flight of stairs off the entryway and saw a carved wooden door cracked open. He peeked his head in and saw a fantastic suite complete with a sitting area and small kitchen. There was a bedroom that faced the corner canals and a bathroom with the biggest tub he'd seen so far in Italy.

"Mine," he said, pulling the thick velvet drapes back to look out the windows. "So, so mine, Tiny."

Ben wandered back to the stairwell and up to the second floor, but the massive arched doors were locked. He poked around the ground floor a little more. It was well maintained, had a surprisingly updated kitchen, but wasn't anything shocking. Another bedroom and what looked like a utility room of some kind. Laundry facilities and gardening tools mainly. Ben's suite was the only room with air-conditioning, so he tossed his bags in the wardrobe and collapsed on the bed.

– ⊕ –

TENZIN landed in the courtyard of the Venice house just after dark to the echo of Louis Armstrong singing

"Hello, Dolly!" coming from the hall on the ground floor. The turntable had been dragged out of the utility room and a pile of old records sat on the table next to it. The colored lanterns were lit and the gate to the canal was swung open. A wine bottle was open on the lacquered table, and Ben was lying stretched on the chaise facing the canal, a glass of wine dangling from his fingers as he watched the shadows of the gondolas pass.

She sat across from him and grabbed for his glass of wine, throwing her legs over the round arm of the rattan chair Silvio must have bought recently, probably when she told him to expect guests.

"Does Silvio know you're playing his records?" she asked as the needle started "Mack the Knife."

"Me and Silvio"—Ben held up his fingers and crossed the first two—"we're like this, T."

Tenzin started laughing at the lazy, half-lidded expression on his face. It wasn't often Ben let himself become intoxicated. When he did, she had to admit she found it entertaining. She sipped the wine and recognized a familiar vintage.

"I see you discovered my wine," she said.

"I moved a few cases to my suite." He sat up and kicked his legs out, grabbing his glass back from her fingers. "I figured you'd want to share. Tenzin, this place is amazing."

She looked around and nodded. "I like it."

"No, no, no. You don't *like* a house like this." He waved a hand toward the canal. "This is *la dolce vita*. This is a house you escape to as often as you can."

She shrugged. "I come here more often than you might guess. Venice is very peaceful at night."

"That's good. I'm glad. I'm glad you come here." He stared at her, his eyes heavy-lidded, his mouth spread in a lazy smile. "Peaceful places are important."

She laughed. "You're drunk."

He slid off the chaise and scooted over to her, sliding his knees across the polished marble.

"Maybe a little." He leaned his elbows next to her and leaned his chin on his hands. "Do you mind?"

She mussed his curls, damp from the muggy Venetian air. "Of course not."

He laid his head on the arm of her chair and closed his eyes. She was a little worried he was going to fall asleep until his ears perked up at the sound of a simple piano melody from the record player.

Ben stood, unfolding his rangy frame with the grace of the slightly buzzed, and held out his hand.

Tenzin shook her head.

"Yes," he insisted, tugging on her hand until she rose to her feet. "You have to."

"It's my house."

"And it's Louis singing 'A Kiss to Build a Dream On.' On a record player." He swung her into his arms and began to lead her around the entry hall. "In the most perfect house in Venice. We have to dance."

She gave up and let him slide one arm around her waist. "What is this?"

"This is... kind of a drunken foxtrot," he said. "Don't question it. Just let me lead."

She laughed when they slid a little too close to the canal steps and Ben swung her back at the last minute. "Just don't lead us into the water!"

He whispered, "Shhhhh."

Ben kept them away from the canal. They swayed as the song crackled in the air, the singer's voice rasping over the smooth trumpet and piano. She felt Ben sigh deeply and pull her closer as the trumpet rose in chorus. He hummed under his breath and continued to spin slowly around the checkerboard floor. Tenzin heard a gondolier outside singing along, his voice raised as he passed the dock and spied them dancing.

"*Bacialo!*" the gondolier called with a laugh. "Kiss him!"

Before Ben could respond, Tenzin floated up and pressed a fleeting kiss to his open mouth.

"Shhhh," she whispered. "Don't spoil it."

Ben smiled his sweet, lazy grin and turned them in another circle.

It was a crystal moment.

A balmy summer night in Venice, the water lapping quietly at the dock as a beautiful boy danced with her under colored lanterns. A slow turn and whirl that reminded Tenzin she was alive. After everything... she was alive. She tucked the dance into a corner of her mind, next to the scattering of other crystal memories.

A baby's laughter.

The feeling of stars inside her.

A gentle brush of paint over bare skin.

A familiar face stamped on the boy in front of her.

An unexpected dance on a warm summer night.

The song wound down, and Ben dipped her back until her hair swept the marble. He slowly raised her up and hugged her tight. "Thank you," he sighed out, "for making me come here."

"You're welcome."

"I needed this."

"I know."

"Yeah," he said, laying his cheek on the top of her head as "Takes Two to Tango" came on the record. "You always seem to, Tiny."

"That's because I am very old and wise."

"And I'm kinda young and stupid sometimes."

She pulled back and looked up at him. "We all were. Even me."

He shook his head. "Nope. Don't believe you."

Ben started to move her to the music again. The wine must have been wearing off because his movements were just a little tighter, his feet a little faster.

"Where did you learn how to dance?"

"Caspar insisted," Ben said, spinning her around with ease. "Told me I'd thank him some day."

"And have you?"

"Many times. Girls love a good dancer."

"So, are you finally relaxed?"

"That depends." He pulled her to his chest and tipped her chin up. "Are you going to introduce me to your forger?"

Tenzin smiled. "I knew you'd figure it out."

– ⊕ –

A YOUNGER, less grumpy version of Silvio picked them up at the dock at midnight. The young man, whom Tenzin introduced as Claudio, kept the boat's motor almost silent until they were well away from San Marco. Speeding into utter blackness, Ben tried not to panic and instead enjoyed the whipping wind on his face as the wood-paneled boat crossed the dark lagoon.

"Where are we going?" he shouted.

"Murano."

"The island of glassblowers?"

"It's not just glass. But the glass helps. Nobody notices his forges there."

Forges. Of course. You couldn't fake medieval coins with a regular art forger, you needed a metalsmith. Someone who could pour the metal and create the dies for the coins. You'd need an engraver too.

"Tenzin?" He switched to Mandarin. "Do you actually have these coins?"

"Of course. I've had them for around four hundred years. Took them from the Neapolitan treasury ages ago."

"So you stole them?"

She shrugged. "Define *steal*."

That sounded like a conversation he'd need more wine for. "The manual you took from Perugia. Was it for your forger's benefit or yours?"

"Mine. Oscar has been doing this for a long time. I

just wanted to check his work. Don't mention the manual to him. He'd be offended."

"Wouldn't dare."

The moon peeked from behind the clouds and lit up the lagoon. Ben tried not to notice how fast they were going since Claudio looked bored. This was clearly a familiar route for the young Venetian.

"The museum," she said. "Did you go like I asked?"

"I did."

"Several of Oscar's copies are in there," Tenzin said.

"So he's good."

"He's the best."

Ben could see tiny lights in the distance. The flat outline of Murano appeared in the sliver of moonlight. The small collection of islands had become the home of all Venetian glassmakers in the thirteenth century when they were forced off the main island by fears of fire. Since then, Murano had swelled and waned in power. Now it was part of Venice, but Ben knew at one time it had its own government. Even minted its own coinage.

"How old is Oscar?" he asked.

Tenzin shrugged. "Ask Oscar."

Yeah, that was likely.

"I first heard of him in the seventeenth century," Tenzin said. "He already had a very good reputation as a metalsmith. Water vampire, of course. Most Venetians are. He designed a piece of jewelry for me around the time I bought my house here. We've been... associates since then."

"So he's at least five hundred years old."

"I'd estimate around six. He was young when I met him, but not that young."

Ben nodded and tucked the information away. Venice in the seventeenth century would have been in decline as an economic and cultural power, but it was still plenty wealthy. Tenzin must have paid someone off handsomely to buy a home in San Marco.

"We'll go to his workshop tonight so you can meet him. He told me the job is about half done. He'll need another week at least before we can return the coins to Alfonso."

"You mean give him the fakes?" He shook his head. "Do you really have the tarì? Or was this whole thing a ruse?"

"Would I lie to you? Of course I have them. How else could Oscar have reproduced them? I like them, and I don't want to give them back. Why should I when I can hire Oscar to make some very nice fakes for Alfonso? I even found some North African gold to duplicate the originals."

"Tenzin, that's not the— Wait, you had a stash of North African gold just lying around?"

"Yes."

He let out a slow breath. "Sometimes I want to be you when I grow up, then I think about your tenuous grasp on sanity and remind myself it wouldn't be a good idea."

She leaned her head back and closed her eyes. The wind whipped her hair around her head. She wasn't wearing braids, so the mass of it rose like a black cloud behind her.

"Sanity," she said, "is vastly overrated."

"Is it really worth pissing off the Mad Duke to keep some old coins? Especially when Gio asked us to tread carefully in Naples? Are they worth *that* much money?"

"No." She sat up and squinted. "That's not the point."

"What is the point?"

"They're mine. I don't give people things that are mine. Especially if I don't like those people."

"But you'll go to all this trouble to forge duplicates for him?"

A smile quirked her lips. "I will enjoy his look of triumph when he holds the fakes. That will be very satisfying."

"Because you'll be laughing internally?"

"Yes."

"You're twisted, Tiny. So very twisted."

"That's what keeps me alive." She leaned forward as the boat approached the islands. Instead of pulling into the main canal, Claudio turned northeast and headed along the outer edge of Murano, slowing to putter past tiny docks where local boats bobbed in the chop. He pulled up to an unmarked set of steps near a redbrick wall.

"Three a.m.?" Claudio asked.

"We'll be here between three and four," Tenzin said. "Is that enough time?"

"Of course." Claudio grinned. "The boat can always go faster."

"Don't scare the boy. I can fly back if time gets short."

Tenzin floated out of the boat and Ben leapt across to the closest dry step.

"Thanks, Claudio."

"See you later," the young man called in English.

Tenzin took Ben's hand and led him down narrow pitch-black streets. Within minutes they were standing outside a small warehouse, its high windows glowing with a red-gold light.

Tenzin knocked once, then pushed the door open. They walked in to see a large, open workshop with a glowing-red forge at one end, racks of tools and equipment across the opposite wall, and a large worktable at the other. A worktable where a black-haired vampire held a woman sprawled. She was half-undressed and her hand clutched his long hair.

"Oscar!" Tenzin yelled.

The vampire's head rose, blood dripping from his lips and his fangs bared.

"You're late," he growled. His hands still pinned the woman down, but she was struggling.

Ben's lip curled and he reached for the knife at his waist. Tenzin put a hand out, halting him.

"I'm paying you to mint coins, not have sex with your engraver. Let Ruby go and show me what's finished."

Chapter Six

RUBY SMACKED OSCAR'S MASSIVE SHOULDER. "Let me up, you beast. And get your hands out of my knickers. You got no sense of propriety, you don't. Sorry, Tenzin!"

Ben turned and faced the forge. "Maybe we should have waited for them to answer the door, huh, Tiny?"

"Why?"

"I forget I ask this of the woman who regularly climbs in my bed to stare at me while I sleep."

"You make it sound creepy, when really I'm just impatient."

Ruby continued to berate Oscar as she dressed. The old vampire muttered something under his breath and she quieted. Then he walked to the forge and waved them over.

"This gold," he said, motioning to a small table. "It's very soft."

"It should be the same composition as the originals," Tenzin said, picking up a button of gold from a shallow pan of sand where a row of buttons had been poured. She dropped it in the bucket nearby.

"It is," Oscar said.

Ben couldn't quite place Oscar's accent. He didn't sound or look Italian. Ben was guessing Spanish, but what would a Spanish glassmaker be doing in Murano? He had a large, smooth scar up the side of his neck, and his head was square as a block. Heavy black hair curtained a face that wasn't handsome but might be called compelling.

Oscar took a pair of clippers and snipped at the row of gold buttons, trimming them into neat rounds as he dropped them in the water. "The softness of this particular alloy means we'll have to do more deformation with the finished pieces than I originally planned."

"You saw the originals I brought. I trust your skills."

"I want some of the trimmings from the reproductions."

Tenzin cocked her head and watched him work. "No."

"I want them," Oscar said, dropping the trimmed gold into a small crucible where he'd melt it down again to make more buttons. Ben could see another pan of sand with round indentations where the smith would pour the next batch of molten gold. "I'm willing to subtract the value out of my fee. I'll even pay above market."

Now Tenzin looked curious. "Why?"

"I want it for a project. That's all you need to know," Oscar said. "Can we work something out or not?"

Tenzin said, "Fine. I'll talk to you about it when the coins are done."

"Good." He nodded toward Ruby and continued trimming. "She has the last two die sets done."

"Excellent."

Ben and Tenzin walked back to the worktable where Ruby was still tucking in her shirt. "Sorry about that, Tenzin."

"Forget about it," Tenzin said. "Ruby, Ben. Ben, Ruby."

"Oh, oi," Ruby said, dark brown eyes sparkling in her round face. She looked African, but every syllable she spoke screamed London. Ben liked her smile, even when he caught the edge of tiny fangs peeking from her lips. "Pleasure to meet you, Ben."

Not a human. Interesting.

"Nice to meet you too." He held out a hand and she took it immediately. Ben was guessing Ruby was fairly young. Her mannerisms and slang said newly turned, and her hair was cut in a stylish, short afro held back with a deep purple scarf.

"So you're the engraver?" he asked.

"I am now!" She grinned. "Oscar taught me the engraving bit. I was an art student before... before."

"She's good," Oscar growled across the room. "She'll be better than me with practice."

"And this was very good practice," she said, pulling up the heavy metal dies with intricate carvings on the face. "Now keep in mind, the actual dies would have degraded over years of use, but we don't have time for that. These are the new ones, but like the other two sets, Oscar'll heat 'em and cool 'em a few times to soften up the edges before we strike the actual coins."

Tenzin nodded as if that all made sense. Ben was quickly catching up.

86

The original coins were over eight hundred years old. They would be scarred and deformed from time. Though gold didn't deteriorate like silver or bronze, some marks of age would be inevitable. The original coin dies used to strike them would have had variations too. So after producing the imitations, Ruby and Oscar were going to have to age them. Each coin would have to be just a little different, or the ruse would be obvious.

Ben picked up a die. Crude Arabic inscriptions around a central circle. "Are these supposed to be... What language is this?"

"The original Norman tarì were imitations of gold coins minted by Arab rulers," Tenzin said. "So they had Arabic or Kufic inscriptions."

"So the original tarì are copies of other coins?"

"In a sense," Tenzin said. "They were made of gold and the size was convenient. That's why they became popular for trading. Nobody much cared who struck them as long as their value held."

"So... we're making copies of coins that were already copies of other coins?" he asked.

Ruby laughed. "It's all so delightfully twisted, ain't it?"

Ben shook his head. "That somehow makes me feel better, but I'm not sure why. Ruby, this work looks amazing. I'm no coin expert, but you're really talented."

"Thank you very much, Ben."

Tenzin was looking at each and every engraving. "I concur. This is excellent work. Oscar has taught you well."

"Means a lot coming from you," Ruby said. "Thanks. I have a batch just out of the tumbler if you'd like to see 'em. Haven't been treated, but they're softened up."

Tenzin nodded. "Let's see."

Ruby took them to a round metal cylinder turned on an angle. "I'd use a proper tumbler for lapidary, but since we're going for a mix of wear, we didn't want anything too even. I mocked up this crude one with a hand turner, and we've been using all sorts of textures for grit. Sand. Polishing compound. Even rocks and metal bits. Small batches. Nothing too regular." She opened the side door and pulled out a coin from the milky liquid within. "Take a look at that then."

Tenzin held the coin in her palm, feeling the weight, then she flipped it end over end and caught it in the air. She held it up to the light and inspected it, then handed it to Ben and reached for another coin.

"It's good," she said. "The weight and wear look perfect. The client hasn't seen the originals in at least four hundred years, so he's not going to be crystal clear on what they look like. No photographic evidence exists, so we just have to get close."

Ruby nodded. "That's what Oscar said too. Mostly we wanted them to have the right wear."

"And the patina?"

Ruby tilted her head toward Oscar. "He's in charge of that. With the copper content of this alloy, I'm thinking liver of sulfur might be involved, but maybe waxes too. Not sure what he has in mind."

"It will look authentic," Oscar shouted. "How I make

it that way is my business."

"Fine," Tenzin shouted back. "And you're about half-done?" she asked Ruby.

The young vampire nodded. "Give us another week or so."

Oscar yelled over the roar of the forge as he put another crucible in to heat. "Ruby will bring them to your house on Thursday night."

Ruby's face lit up. "Really, Oz? All the way to the main island?"

Oscar grunted. "Just stay out of sight. Tenzin, leave. You're distracting Ruby from her work."

"Fine." Tenzin walked over and punched his shoulder. The stocky man glared at her.

"What was that for?" he shouted.

"Just because you're a bastard," Tenzin said. "Don't bite your woman unless she likes it, Oscar. I have ways of finding out."

"She likes it." Oscar's eyes flicked up to Ben. "What's this one, anyway?"

"Him?" Tenzin glanced over her shoulder. "He's my publicist."

Oscar narrowed his eyes. "Right. Keep him away from Ruby."

"Ben's trustworthy. He's not going to poach your woman, you paranoid ass."

"She's an investment."

Tenzin punched him again. "Such a bastard."

– ⊕ –

THURSDAY night, Ruby turned up just after dark in Claudio's small boat. With her was a battered leather briefcase that must have weighed more than a bit, because the boat rocked when she hoisted it onto the steps.

"Thanks, Claudio!" she said, waving at the young man before he disappeared down the canal. Then Ruby planted her hands on her hips and looked at Ben. "Gelato?"

"Uh..." He set down the book he'd been reading. "I think we have some."

"I don't care if you have some here," she said, grabbing his hand. "I want to go *out*. See the city. Get a drink. And definitely eat some gelato."

"Okay." Ben laughed and let her pull him down the entry hall. "Don't get off work much, huh?"

"Ugh," she groaned. "Oscar's great, right? I don't mean to whinge on. But he's really overprotective. Very possessive, you know? I just need to get out a bit. I'm not nine hundred like some people."

Ben tucked that one away and went to grab the key for the door. "Come on then. I'll be your trusted escort through the city."

Ruby winked. "Know every nook and cranny, do you?"

"Not quite, but I'm getting there."

He glanced up and wondered if he needed to tell

Tenzin they were going. Then he spied the heavy briefcase sitting on the stairs.

"Is that...?"

"A bloody fortune in reproduced Sicilian tarì? Yes, it is." Ruby smiled. "And rather expertly reproduced if I say so myself."

"Let me take it up to Tenzin," he said. "Let her know we're going out."

Ruby was strolling along the entry hall, examining the marbles. "So you've got a mummy too, eh?"

"A mummy?" Ben resisted the urge to break into hysterical laughter. "No, not exactly."

He hoisted the briefcase and climbed the stairs to the second level, knocking before he pushed the door open.

Tenzin was stretched out on a thick Persian rug at the end of the *pòrtego*, the grand entry hall on the main floor of the house. She was on her back, reading a book in front of the arched floor-to-ceiling windows that lined the front of the house. During the day, they were covered with a heavy red velvet drape, but at night they reflected the lights glittering across the canal.

The rest of the *pòrtego* was sparsely furnished and looked more like a gallery than a room. The terrazzo floors were a soft gold color and the walls were covered in a red Venetian plaster, but the ceilings were the tallest in the house, which meant they were the most comfortable for Tenzin, who preferred flying to walking when possible.

Ben tapped on the door again and she waved him in.

"Ruby's here," she said, putting the book on the

ground.

He walked over and set the briefcase down next to her. "Yep."

Tenzin grinned. "She brought the coins."

"Is this the part where I pour them over you in a river of gold while you laugh maniacally? Because I'm going to be honest, this bag is heavy and I'm wondering how comfortable that would be."

"No, no, no." She rolled over and grabbed the briefcase. "Ah," she said, peering inside. "Lovely."

It wasn't a river, but when Tenzin poured out the perfectly reproduced tarì over the rich wool of the Persian rug, Ben had to admit...

It was hot.

She spread them with her hands, a small sea of intricately etched gold coins scattering over the red, blue, and ochre of the rug. Ben knelt next to her and picked one up. The patina looked identical to the examples he'd seen online. Even to his experienced eye, the coins looked hundreds of years old.

"Amazing," he said.

"Come on," Tenzin said, pushing the coins into a pile. "It's not enough for a bed, but you can use it for a pillow."

He laughed. "A pillow?"

"Just..." She stood and pushed him down to the rug. "Do it. Everyone should lie on a big pile of gold at least once in their life, Benjamin."

"Did you read that on a motivational poster somewhere?"

"No, but maybe someone should make one with that on it. I find gold very motivating."

Ben lay down on the rug and put his head on the pile of gold coins, staring at the ceiling. The beams had been painted with tiny decorative elements in red and lapis blue. The rug was soft at his back. And the pile of gold coins...

Tenzin lay down next to him. "It isn't very comfortable, is it?"

"No." He picked up a coin and flipped it in the air. "Sleeping on gold does have a certain appeal though."

"Yes." Tenzin scooped a handful and let the coins run through her fingers. "Gold always does."

The cool metal warmed to his neck as he lay on it. "I think that's what it is," he murmured.

"What?"

"The gold. It's... warm. It's precious metal, but it's not cold. Diamonds are hard and cold. Platinum always feels mechanical to me. But gold..." He picked up a coin and balanced it on his nose. "Never tarnishes. It doesn't break; it bends. It's warm. More human than other precious metals or gems."

He turned to see her watching him with a smile flirting at the corner of her mouth. "What?"

Tenzin said, "I've always wondered when you'd find it. It's an honor to be here when you did."

"What are you talking about?"

"Your one true love." Tenzin laughed and rolled away when he grabbed for her. "Should I leave you alone?"

"Shut up."

"Wait, I can't leave you alone. Your one true love needs to go in the safe." She flipped a coin at him, and he caught it just before it hit his face. "Kiss your true love good-bye, Benjamin."

"You're ridiculous."

"You're the one philosophizing about gold."

He filled a hand with the coins and let them pour out onto the rug again, delighting in the soft sound. "Do you blame me?"

"Me?" She rolled to her knees. "Never." Tenzin flipped a coin up, caught it, and kissed it before she tossed it in the bag. "Not when I'm guilty of the same thing. Like recognizes like, my Benjamin."

He tossed coin after coin in the leather satchel, listening to each one clink. "Ruby is still here. Wants to go out for a drink and some ice cream. You want to join us?"

She wouldn't want to join them.

"No"—Tenzin confirmed his suspicion—"just be careful with her. Oscar is very possessive."

"Yeah, I got that." He frowned. "Everything all right there?"

"It's none of my business." Tenzin shrugged. "The girl doesn't appear to be unhappy."

"And if she was?"

Tenzin raised an eyebrow in speculation. "Ask her."

"Fine. Be cryptic." He rolled up to his knees. "You want to finish this and I'll play host?"

Tenzin's eyes danced. "That girl knows the city better

than either of us, I'd wager. Don't let her fool you. She's smart and she's not nearly as innocent as she comes across."

"Probably not." He shrugged. "But she's fun. We won't stay out too late."

"Nothing stays open late enough to worry about," she said. "This isn't Naples."

"Very true."

The thing that delighted Tenzin most about Venice was the very thing that annoyed Ben. It was too quiet at night. There was little to no nightlife unless you took a boat out to the Lido or trolled the tourist areas along the Grand Canal. Still, he'd found a good gelato place just around the corner on the Calle de la Mandola, and there was a bar not too far from it in Campo Sant'Angelo that served a nice selection of cocktails where they could sit if they wanted.

Ruby was waiting for him when he came down the stairs. "So, permission granted?"

Ben shook his head and cocked an arm out for her to take. "Come on, you brat. Let's find someplace you can let your hair down."

– ⊕ –

THEY were sitting in the Campo Sant'Angelo and most of the square was empty. Ben and Ruby had the place to themselves, aside from a small group of what looked like retirees who were chatting in German on the other side of the restaurant. The moon had risen and the night was warm. The wine wasn't great, but it wasn't bad either.

The company, however, was stellar.

"So tell me about vampires in Venice," Ben said. "How long have you lived here?"

Ruby cocked her head. "Ten years now? Almost eleven, I suppose." She grinned and the points of her fangs peeked from her lips. "I came on holiday and I never left."

"Intentional?"

"Very much not."

"But you've stayed."

"Well, I've got Oscar, don't I?" she said. "Can't leave him. Not until he gets bored with me."

Ben's protective instincts pricked. "Do you *want* to leave?"

Ruby winked at him. "You're adorable, you know that? It's not what you're thinking. But when I first came, it wasn't under ideal circumstances. In fact, Oscar's the one who brought me up in front of the council here."

"So there's a council? Not just one VIC?"

"VIC?"

Ben shrugged. "My shorthand for vampire in charge."

"Ha!" Ruby laughed. "That's brilliant. Yeah, there's a council. It's not big. For an old city, there's not as many of our kind as you'd think."

Ben thought for a moment. "No nightlife."

She pointed a finger at him. "Right in one. That's it. There's a larger population on *terraferma*, but in the old city? Not many anymore. And the ones here are more like Oscar. Old, ornery, and like keeping to themselves."

"And he's the one who took you to them?"

"Long story, but yeah. And I'm grateful he did. What did I know about any of this, eh?" She looked around. "I would've turned these canals bloody if I'd had my way. Oscar reined me in. Looked after me."

"And you work for him."

She grinned. "Among other things. No worries, Benny. He's not a bad sort. I'm happy enough."

"So you're settled here?"

Ruby snorted. "God, no. I'd love to get out. Travel the world. That's what I was doing before I turned, you know? I'm an artist. I can't stay in one place forever, can I?" She sipped her wine. "But I've got time. Gobs and gobs of it now. So we'll see. I'm here now."

"Well"—he took his card out of his pocket—"if you ever make your way to America—and I'm still alive—give me a call, huh?"

Ruby took the card and put it in a pocket. "I'll do that. So you and Tenzin?"

He shrugged. "It's complicated."

"Friends?"

"Yes," he said. "Always."

"She's a bit of a legend, isn't she? Got the creeps the first time I met her. Stories Oscar told made my hair stand on end." She fingered her tight curls. "Even more than it is now. And that's saying something."

Ben smiled. "Yeah, I've heard a few of them too."

A chime sounded in Ben's pocket, and he pulled out his phone.

"The docks near San Samuele," he said. "Sounds like Claudio's picking both of us up there at midnight."

"Both of us?"

"That's what he says." He tucked his phone away.

"Maybe Tenzin went out to your place."

"Could be." She lifted her wineglass. "We should probably get going. I know the way."

Ten minutes later, they walked through the twisted streets of San Marco again, their footsteps echoing in the deserted city. If it hadn't been so empty, Ben would never have spotted their shadows as they crossed the Campo Santo Stefano.

"We've got company," he said under his breath, knowing Ruby would hear. "Just passing the library now."

Ruby's head whipped around and back so fast he could barely see it. "Vampires. I don't recognize them."

Ben's eyes glinted. "Shall we see how well they know the city?"

"Can you keep up?"

He grinned. "Not even a little."

Ruby ran.

She kept to human-ish speed, but Ben still had the devil's time keeping her in sight. She sped past the church on the south end of the campo and ducked right across a small bridge, almost losing him in the maze of streets.

Their vampire trackers stayed with them. They were little more than shadows, but they drew nearer to Ben, bolder than they were with Ruby. They knew he was human.

He ran past an alleyway and felt an arm reach out and grab him. Ruby pulled him next to her while Ben struggled to catch his breath.

"What?" he panted.

Ruby looked troubled. "If they were residents, I'd

know them. If they were simply curious, they'd have left us by now."

Ben heard them slinking down the street. If there had been any other foot traffic, he'd have never have heard their silent feet, but they were utterly alone. His pulse hammering, he looked toward the mouth of the alley. When he looked back, Ruby's eyes were narrowed on the pulse in his throat.

He snapped his fingers in her face and she looked up, baring her fangs at him.

"Not the time," he whispered.

She was right. These vampires were following them for some reason, and Ben was guessing he didn't want to find out.

"Pretend you're biting me," he said, tugging her closer.

"Do I have to pretend?"

"Do it!" he hissed.

The vampires crossed the alley just as Ruby bent her head to his neck. They paused, watching them.

A low laugh and one said to another, "This one likes all kinds, eh?"

The minute Ben heard the distinctive accent of Naples, he jerked back. He met the eyes of one of the vampires from Alfonso's court in the dim streetlamp, then he glanced at Ruby.

Oh shit.

Chapter Seven

"THEY CAN'T SEE US TOGETHER," he said. "Ruby, they're from Naples."

"Got it."

With a quick flip, Ruby climbed up the wall, the tips of her fingers clinging to the bricks before she leapt on the two vampires at the mouth of the alley. Ben drew his knife and ran for the one Ruby hadn't landed on, cursing himself the whole time.

Man versus vampire rarely went his way.

His advantage? The vampire wasn't looking to get away and didn't want to kill him. Ben knew that any of Alfonso's court seeing him with Oscar's apprentice would be bad news.

The vampire circled him, fangs down, his head cocked curiously at the human he'd been tracking. He said nothing. His dark hood was drawn up around his face, but Ben recognized him. He recognized them both.

Ruby had one vampire's face shoved into the cobblestones while the other circled Ben. If it had been faster, they'd both have been dizzy.

"What do you want?" Ben asked. Shit, shit, shit. Ruby could keep that one down, but this one looked old and smart. He was no match for a vampire. His survival strategy consisted of avoiding violence and relying on charm and connections. "Does Alfonso know you're here?"

"He sent us to watch you." The vampire glanced at Ruby. "You keep curious company, Tenzin's human."

"What can I say?" he said. "I make friends easily."

"But your choice of friends... this says much."

"You think so?" Ben held up his hand, letting the vampire see his knife. "Listen, I'm prey, but I'm not easy prey. Is this really worth it? I met a cute girl. We went out for a drink."

The vampire laughed. "You're not as smart as they say if you think I'd believe—" His words were cut off with his head, which fell to the side and plopped on the cobblestones with a wet thunk a second before Tenzin landed next to Ben.

He let out a slow breath. "Tenzin. What. The. Hell?"

"I told Alfonso not to send anyone to watch us," she said, bending down to the one Ruby held. "Is that why you're here? To watch me?"

Ruby let go of the vampire's throat.

"Yes," he choked out.

"Filomena or Alfonso?"

"Alfonso."

"Thank you," Tenzin said graciously. "I appreciate your honesty. I will give you a swift death like your friend."

Ben's hand shot out. "Tenzin—"

She was already gone. She'd lifted the vampire from the ground, shoving Ruby off him, and flown straight up. Ben heard scuffling on the top of the nearest building, then quiet.

"Fuck me," Ruby breathed out. "She *is* scary as 'ell."

Ben sighed. "Yeah, she is. And she always kills them before I can ask the questions I want."

Ruby patted his shoulder. "They died clean."

For following orders, his conscience complained. He tried to ignore it. If Alfonso had ordered Ben dead, those vampires wouldn't have thought twice about following those orders too. He'd seen that truth in their eyes. They could have taken Ruby with ease if Ben hadn't been around to distract one of them. They'd have killed her and not batted an eye.

Ben looked at the wall Ruby had crawled up. "How did you do that?"

"Do what? Climb the wall?"

"You looked like fucking Spider-Man for a minute there."

She smiled. "It's not easy, but you could teach yourself if you want. It's called parkour. I started studying it while I was still human. When I became a vamp... way cooler."

"Parkour?"

"Parkour."

Tenzin landed in the alley again, a delicate spray of blood across her cheek. She walked over, nodded at Ruby, and picked up the head and the body of the other vampire. He could see her favorite sword, a curved Mongolian saber designed for combat on horseback, strapped to her back. Tenzin never went anywhere without that sword.

"Thank you," Tenzin said to Ruby when she landed again. "I am in your debt for protecting Benjamin."

"Hey," he said. "Standing right here."

"No problem," Ruby said. "And he holds his own pretty well."

Tenzin sighed. "I am hoping he gets over this desire to be human. He's much more vulnerable as a mortal."

Ruby laughed.

"That's enough, Tiny." Ben looked up at the side of the building Ruby had crawled up. "What are we going to do with these guys?"

"They were both from Naples, and Oscar would have told me if anyone from Alfonso's court had permission to enter the city. They were fair game if any of the Venetians got them anyway."

"I'll tell Oscar they were threatening me," Ruby said. "He'll smooth over anything with the council. Venetians may be a quiet lot, but they don't like trespassers." Ruby nodded at the roof of the building. "You can dump their bodies out in the lagoon."

"Oh, I know a few places," Tenzin said. "I do so love that splash. You two, get to the boat. I'll meet you in Murano."

– ⊕ –

TEN minutes of listening to Oscar berate Ruby was more than enough for Ben. He was ready to murder the cranky old vampire. Though Oscar didn't raise a hand to Ruby, he beat her with his voice.

"Enough," Tenzin said. "I don't need to be here for this. Punish your woman on your own time, Oscar."

Oscar turned and bared his fangs at Tenzin before he turned back to Ruby. "Go to your room," he snarled. "I don't want to see you until tomorrow night."

Ruby's normally vivacious expression was gone. Her face was a mask. She looked down and nodded quietly before she left the workroom.

Ben started. "Ruby—"

"Shut up," Tenzin said, slapping her hand against his chest. "Shut. Up. Oscar, we're leaving."

"I hope you like the coins," he said, throwing his hammer down and shutting off his forge. "Because they're the last job I'm going to do for you, Tenzin."

"Fine," she said. "I apologize if I caused any trouble."

"Don't bring that human around Ruby again."

"Just remember I have ways of knowing," she said in a low voice. "Never again, Oscar."

"Out of my house!" he shouted. "And don't come back!"

Tenzin pushed Ben out the door and down the street toward the dock.

"He is going to beat her," Ben hissed. "Hurt her. And you're going to just let him?"

"Oscar is not going to beat Ruby," Tenzin said. "He's going to shout and rail, but that's all he's going to do."

Ben scrambled into the boat and glared at her as she floated in. "Oh yeah? How do you know?"

"Because he almost killed a friend of mine once," Tenzin said calmly. "A woman who had been his lover.

He lost his temper when she left him."

Ben sat down, shocked into silence.

Ruby... He felt sick to his stomach for leaving her there.

"So I cut Oscar's balls off and stabbed a knife through his neck." She held up two fingers an inch apart. "Very close to his spine. His balls took a long time to grow back. He won't hit Ruby."

Ben shuddered. They rode in silence all the way back to San Marco, then Claudio dropped them off and sped into the night with a casual nod.

"Tenzin," Ben said.

"What?"

"Oscar... Is that really the last job he'll do for you?" As much as Ben might not have liked Oscar at the moment, he was a good contact. A great artist, and a discreet one from what Tenzin had said. Losing his skills would be a shame.

Tenzin frowned as if she was confused. "The last...? Oh." She waved her hand and sat on the chair in the entry hall. "I think he says that every time we work together. This is not unusual. He'll be fine. He'll be doting on Ruby by tomorrow night and best friends with me when I deliver a shipment of that gold he likes as a bonus."

"What are they?" He finally asked the question that had been bugging him ever since they left Murano. "Why would she stay with him? He treats her like a child."

"Well, how should he treat her?"

"Not like a child!"

"But she *is* a child. To him, she's a child. Oscar is not her father or her sire, but he is her superior. And her lover. In his mind, that makes Ruby *his*. You may not understand it—"

"I sure as hell don't understand it, and I don't understand why she'd stay with him when he treats her like that."

"Ben…" Tenzin closed her eyes and sighed. "Most vampire relationships are not like your aunt and uncle's. You should have learned this by now. There are no saints in this world. No one acts completely out of the goodness of their heart. There is always self-interest involved. Oscar protects Ruby. Cares about her in his own way. Ruby feeds Oscar and learns valuable skills from him. They both get something from the other, or it would not be balanced."

"That doesn't look like a balanced relationship to me."

"He is in charge of her, *but* she gets his protection. It's balanced."

"And she's supposed to be satisfied with that?"

"They're not *mates*, Benjamin. Will they be someday?" Tenzin shrugged. "Perhaps. Probably not."

Ben sat on the chaise and reached for the bottle of wine he'd been drinking hours before when Ruby had first shown up with the gold. He pulled the cork out and drank directly from the bottle, then passed it to Tenzin.

"So how does it end?" he asked.

She took a long drink. "None of your business."

"But—"

"Not everything comes to a happy end, Benjamin." She reached over and patted his hand. "Remember that. We're vampires."

BEN drove to Rome the next day. Tenzin didn't trust the coins on the train and neither did Benjamin, so he started early, rented a junky tourist car, and made the six-hour trip on his own. He pulled into Residenza di Spada just a couple of hours before sunset and grabbed a nap before Tenzin arrived.

When he woke, he was alone, but he could see Tenzin outside his room, perched on the small balcony that overlooked the interior courtyard. He opened the window and heard the quiet buzz of city traffic, not knowing whether the clamor of vehicles was comforting or annoying.

"You're being so well behaved," Ben said as Tenzin floated into his room. Since he couldn't float, he sat on the edge of the bed. "You actually waited for me to wake up this time."

She was frowning and silent.

"What's up?"

"How was your meeting with Filomena before you left Naples?"

"Filomena?" He rubbed the sleep from his eyes as

Tenzin hovered in a corner. "Good, I guess. We flirted. Nothing much happened. But she seemed pretty progressive for a vampire."

"Instant read on her?"

He took a deep breath and lay back, closing his eyes as he thought. "I liked her. She's smart. Doesn't take herself too seriously. I found myself... surprised that she was Alfonso's lieutenant."

"Why?"

"One, she seems too independent for him. Two, he doesn't seem like the type to have an independent thinker as his second-in-command."

"Which tells us..."

He stretched and rolled over. "It tells us she's either got him fooled, or there's more layers to the Mad Duke than we're seeing."

Tenzin nodded and crossed her legs on the end of his bed.

"Do you know who she reminded me of?" Ben finally said.

"Emil Conti?"

"*Yes.*" Ben wasn't surprised Tenzin had picked up Filomena's similarity to the vampire in charge of Rome. "Old but progressive. The Naples court is too insular for her."

"I'm betting she didn't know Alfonso sent two men to follow you."

"I'd bet you're right. She had too much respect for

you to piss you off."

"I think before we meet with Alfonso and give him his gold—"

"You mean, give him *your* gold that you very nicely forged for him?"

"Exactly. I think before we meet with Alfonso again, you should have another meeting with Filomena and... fill her in."

Ben narrowed his eyes. "What kind of trouble are you trying to cause, Tiny?"

"Benjamin, you know I only cause the very best kind of trouble."

Chapter Eight

BEN MET FILOMENA AT THE same restaurant where they'd had a drink before he left Naples. The vicious heat wave had not let up, but the breeze across the bay cooled the evening enough to make things slightly less miserable.

He spotted Filomena walking along the boardwalk. She was wearing a long summer dress that evening, which made Ben wonder where she was hiding her weapons. Wherever they were, he had a feeling he'd have a fun time finding out. It was a shame he had to talk about politics.

"Hey," he said when she came close. "Nice dress." He flipped one of the tarì at her, and her hand shot out to catch it.

Filomena held it in her palm. "Nice gold."

"Did ya miss me?"

"Wouldn't you like to know?"

She sat and slid a hand along his thigh until she'd leaned forward enough to brush his lips with her own. "Hello."

He tasted cherries and smiled against her lips. "Hey, Filomena?"

"Yes?"

"I want to give you a nickname. Can I do that?"

"If you call me baby, it might result in injury."

"No baby." His fingertips slid along her soft shoulder. "I'm going to think about it. I'm just warning you. A nickname is coming."

Filomena pouted. "If only I were too." She sat back and held up the tarì. "You got them."

"We got them. But we had some company—"

"What?" She straightened, all flirtation forgotten. "You had what kind of company?"

"The kind Alfonso sent. Anyone go on vacation lately?"

"That..." She closed her eyes and took a deep breath. "Was Tenzin very angry?"

"She wasn't happy. Which is why I wanted to meet with you before she sees Alfonso again."

"He'll claim he was protecting his interests."

"And she'll claim his sending people to follow her is an indication of distrust. And an insult to her reputation. Which, Filomena, you know it is."

She said nothing, torn between loyalty to her boss and realization that he'd made a significant misstep. "What do you suggest?"

"Would he apologize?"

Filomena snorted. "Never."

"Not even privately?"

"No."

"Then we're at an impasse."

"If..." Filomena's mouth pursed in concentration. "If the vampires who followed you were acting on their own..."

"But they weren't."

"But if they were..." She raised an eyebrow.

"If they were," he said, "it would change things, but they both claimed Alfonso sent them."

She smiled slowly. "But we're terribly dishonest creatures, are we not?"

Ben deliberated.

Tenzin had sent him to find out how much Filomena knew, but Ben knew he could also work this around to his benefit if he played his cards right. Filomena wanted to appease Tenzin and cover her boss's ass. And yet if word got out that Tenzin had allowed Alfonso to track her without consequences, it set a dangerous precedent.

"She'll give him the coins," Ben said, "but she'll need a higher finder's fee. It caused some trouble when she had to take care of them."

It hadn't—they hadn't heard a peep from the council in Venice about the two dead vampires—but Alfonso didn't need to know that.

"Of course," Filomena said. "I'm sure an additional fee could be arranged to compensate you for this unfortunate incident. As long as the transaction was agreed to privately. I'll guarantee the increased fee and the exchange will work out as previously arranged."

Private was a... fluid concept. Gossip in Naples would spread the word that something went down and that Alfonso paid the price for it. Not knowing specifics would allow both Tenzin and Alfonso to save face. On the surface, it was a perfect solution.

So why was a voice in head telling Ben he was

missing something?

"I'll take your proposal back to Tenzin and let you know," he told Filomena. "I'm fairly sure that will be sufficient. And of course, if you didn't know about the scouts, I doubt anyone else did."

A little flattery never hurt.

Filomena's eyes flashed. "I would have known if they did."

They exchanged pleasantries for a few more minutes, but the playful banter had died when Ben mentioned Alfonso's mistake. Filomena's mood had turned from flirtatious to calculating. She chatted with Ben, but her mind was elsewhere.

They finished their wine and bid each other good-bye at the waterfront, and Ben walked back to his hotel alone. When he got to his room, Tenzin was reading a book on his bed.

"Fairly confident I'd be spending tonight alone, were you?"

"You're not alone." She patted his side of the bed without looking up. "You have me. And I'm far more entertaining."

"She didn't know about the scouts," he said, kicking off his shoes and stretching out on the bed. "And she wasn't happy about them."

"Interesting."

"She agreed to a larger finder's fee to compensate for our inconvenience."

Tenzin put down her book. "Well, that was clever of you. Nicely done."

"But she says he won't apologize."

She frowned. "So this is private? No public acknowledgement?"

"No mention from either party. Filomena will arrange the money. I have a feeling Alfonso is using public funds for this. Might not want his people to know how much he's spending to get these back."

"Very... interesting."

"Because?"

She shrugged. "We'll have to see whether this deal you worked out with her actually happens. If the exchange goes as planned... When?"

"Tomorrow night. Midnight."

"If it goes as planned tomorrow—we make the transfer and Alfonso gives us a higher fee privately—that means Filomena is acceding to Alfonso's authority and allowing him to take security steps without her knowledge."

Yeah, Ben had a feeling that *wasn't* going to be the way it went down.

"And if it doesn't go as planned?" he asked.

"Then duck."

– ⊕ –

THEY met two of Filomena's people in front of Alfonso's nightclub the next night. She'd warned Ben that she wouldn't be coming herself, so neither Ben nor Tenzin was surprised. The two younger vampires led them through the popular club, openly baring fangs at humans who laughed and ran from them.

Ben looked around in sudden realization. "They think it's a game."

Tenzin said, "They usually do."

Ben, Tenzin, and their two escorts stepped behind a heavy curtain at the back of the club and descended stone steps where two more vampires guarded the entrance to Alfonso's court. The pulse of music pounded at his back, growing softer as they descended. As one, the two vampires opened the double doors for them and they stepped through, the damp earthen smell assaulting Ben's senses after the smell of cologne, alcohol, and sweat in the club above.

Tenzin walked behind him. He could feel her wary energy in the subtle press of wind against his back. He reached a hand back and gripped hers for a second before he released it. In his other hand, he carried a metal briefcase full of fake Sicilian tarì.

It was heavy, which meant he could use it as a weapon. Not a bad thing to have in your hands when you were walking into a giant den of vampires. The knives at his waist pressed into his skin, reassuring him with their cool presence.

The court was full that night. Dozens of dark-eyed vampires lounged on the steps around Alfonso's throne, others gathered in the shadow of pillars that held up the old Roman ruins. Filomena was one of them, her tall figure clad in a brilliant shirt of blue, yellow, and red. It glowed in the low light. Ben let Tenzin take the lead, coming up behind her, still carrying the gold.

Filomena stepped forward and said, "We welcome your return, Tenzin, daughter of Zhang Guolao. Sired of air. Mated to water, scourge of the Naiman Khanlig. Commander of the Altan Wind. Protector of Penglai Island. Patron goddess of the Holy Mountain, protector and scribe of New Spain. Friend of Don Ernesto Alvarez of Los Angeles." Filomena took a breath. "And we also welcome Benjamin Vecchio, ward of Giovanni Vecchio, scholar and ally of Rome."

As soon as Filomena said his uncle's name, silence fell in the court. He could feel the air in the room shift as vampires turned to stare at him.

Okay, so things were already going sideways.

"Lovely," he muttered. "Always nice to be the center of attention."

Tenzin spoke in Mandarin. "Stay close."

"This is the ward of di Spada?" Alfonso rose to his feet. "In my city?"

Filomena gestured toward Tenzin. "Tenzin is Di Spada's old partner, my lord. You knew that when you hired her. Is it any wonder she brings the assassin's son with her?"

"Not his son," Ben said quietly. "Not that it matters, I guess."

Alfonso was glaring at Filomena. "I will deal with your insubordinate tone later. Tenzin, did you find what I hired you to find?"

Ben held out the briefcase to Tenzin, who took it. He suddenly felt naked and put his hands in his pockets, pressing his forearms against the blades at his sides.

Tenzin said, "I found it. I will expect the fee transferred to my account by the end of this night."

Filomena stepped forward again. "Did you not know that she had found the tarì, my lord? After all, you sent Patricio and Armand to follow the boy when he left your city so you could be kept abreast of their progress."

Suspicious murmurs from the crowd of vampires. Alfonso's lip curled up at his lieutenant.

"Silence, Filomena."

"Where are they?" Filomena asked, pressing forward as a dozen vampires moved to guard her sides. "Have your scouts not returned?"

Aaaaand any hope of getting out of Alfonso's glorified basement fled at that moment.

Ben glanced at Tenzin. Her head was cocked, watching Filomena with narrow eyes.

"What is she doing?" he whispered.

Tenzin said, "She's being very shrewd. Filomena has drawn me in. I can't ignore Alfonso's slight now."

"What?"

Tenzin flexed her shoulder and smiled. "She's maneuvered me into becoming her ally. Clever, clever girl. This just became interesting."

"I really wish you didn't sound so chipper right now."

"But it works out beautifully!"

"How?" Ben hissed. "How does this work out in any way that could be considered beautiful?"

Ben could see factions already forming as over half the vampires in the room drifted toward Filomena while others gathered closer to Alfonso. In truth, the factions had probably lain beneath the surface for months or years. Or centuries.

"You spend the wealth of our city treasury to find a fortune you claim as your own," Filomena said, walking toward the throne. "You put corrupt humans in place and allow them to steal from your own people. What makes you better than the Romans who looted Naples in the first place?"

"I *am* Naples." Alfonso rose to his feet. "And you are nothing."

"I am the woman who will take this city from you!" Filomena said, drawing her sword. "And my people stand behind me."

With a surge, the vampires of Naples met in a clashing roar.

"Now is the time that you duck!" Tenzin yelled, shoving him behind a pillar and throwing the briefcase at his chest. "Here, hold this!"

Ben slid down the pillar, holding the briefcase. "Can't. Breathe."

That swing might have crushed a few ribs, but Ben listened to Tenzin. He had absolutely no dog in this fight, and he did not consider armed combat a fun way to hang out on a Saturday night.

He scrambled to a better location, knowing that in the rush to avoid eternal death most of the vampires had probably forgotten about the giant pile of gold he was holding, but not all of them would. Immortals were nothing if not opportunistic.

Ben noticed the first lurker as the vampire made his way toward the stairs. The stocky brown-haired man spotted Ben from the corner of his eye and grinned.

"Yeah," Ben said. "Can't imagine what you want, buddy."

The vampire jumped on him with stunning speed, reaching for Ben's throat as Ben swung his knife deep into his attacker's gut and pulled up. He twisted the knife around a few times until the vampire let go of his neck.

Quick. Messy. Ben's hands were covered in blood, but his throat and the briefcase were safe. The unexpected attack was enough to deter the vampire, who was only looking for easy prey before he fled. With a snarl, the immortal ran toward the back stairs, holding his bleeding gut.

Tenzin landed beside him. "Are you all right?"

"Yes, but—"

She took off again. Ben tried to make himself invisible while still keeping an eye on the fight.

It was clear that Filomena's allies had come prepared. Most were cutting down Alfonso's friends with quick chops and sweeping strokes from blades while many of Alfonso's allies were unarmed. It was an ambush. Ben saw mostly European blades, but Filomena carried a katana, and Ben even saw a few battle-axes.

Retro.

A few took the time to feed from their enemies, but most of the carnage was practical. Cut down. Take head. Go for the next one.

The second vampire who attacked him tried to grab

him from the side. She launched in Ben's direction and latched on with all four limbs, slamming him to the ground before she attempted to dig in with clawlike fingernails. Ben twisted away, grappling with her superior strength while tossing away a butcher knife she'd stowed on her back.

He managed to roll far enough away to put a hard boot in her neck. The impact stunned her enough that Ben got in another couple of kicks before she hissed and ran away.

He crawled to another corner, dragging the damned briefcase with him. Tenzin was swooping over the heads of the fighters, one of the few air vampires in the room. Most of Filomena's people were, like herself, water vampires. Isolated from easy access to their element, the battle was dirty and bloody and crude.

It was hard to tell how long it lasted. All Ben knew was, by the time the third vampire attacked, he was sick. The smell of blood was thick in the air; he could taste it on his lips. He saw the vampire running and aimed a throwing knife at one eye. He threw it, hit the target, then sent three more into the twitching body before he walked away. He hadn't killed it, but it was on the ground and one knife had gotten close enough to the thing's neck that Ben doubted it would chase him.

"Tenzin!" he shouted.

She landed a few minutes later, her face flushed like a child coming in from play. "Are you hurt?"

"No."

"Is the gold safe?"

"Yes."

She frowned. "Then what's wrong?"

His throat was tight. "Is this almost done? I want to turn over this gold, collect our fee, and go home. Unless someone else is planning to attack us."

Tenzin's eyes took a slow sweep around the room, then she poked her head around the corner and reported, "Filomena has almost killed Alfonso. I think this is close to done."

Ben joined her, craning his neck around the pillar to see Filomena roar, her blouse drenched in blood, two swords in her hands. She whirled and struck at Alfonso, who parried with surprising speed. Alfonso had brute strength going for him, but it was clear who was the better swordsman. Filomena worked Alfonso across the dais until he was bent back over his throne.

"How does the throne feel now, you mad Spanish bastard?" Filomena screamed.

Alfonso tried to roll away, but she brought her blade down on his neck before he could escape. Unfortunately, the blade didn't go clear through, and Alfonso's head listed to the side but didn't quite detach.

Ben winced and looked away.

"Unfortunate," Tenzin said. "She hit him at a difficult angle. She'll get it on the next—ah. Gone now."

The roar of the crowd told him that Filomena's allies clearly considered their side victorious. Since Ben didn't know which bodies belonged to which side, he couldn't judge just by looking at the carnage.

"We done now?" Ben said.

"I believe so."

He crossed his arms and leaned against what was now his favorite pillar, his boot resting on the edge of the briefcase with all the gold tarì. A thought struck him. "Hey, Tiny?"

"Yes?"

"Was Alfonso the only one who ever saw the original coins?"

Tenzin leaned against the pillar next to him. "Other than me, I believe he was."

"So there is now no one who'll be able to..."

"Correct."

He let out a slow breath. "Did you plan this out in advance?"

She shrugged. "Let's just say that it was time for Naples to leap into the twenty-first century. We just gave it a little nudge."

Ben heard Filomena giving some kind of inspirational speech in the background about the new Neapolitan republic and the end of foreign oppression as she stood over the bodies of the vampires she'd killed.

And Ben felt... exhausted.

He picked up the briefcase full of gold, handed it to Tenzin, and walked toward the stairs.

"Where are you going?" she called.

"Home."

The problem was, Ben wasn't quite sure where home was at the moment.

So he went to Tuscany.

Chapter Nine

THE HOUSE IN TUSCANY WAS out in the country, surrounded by olive groves and grapevines. The vines in midsummer were laden with thick-skinned purple fruit and lush green leaves. He walked through the vineyard during the day and ate the sweet, seedy grapes. He brought a blanket into the olive grove and lay in the afternoon shade, reading a book or napping. He ate sandwiches made from the bread and cheese he bought when he rode his old bike into town. He opened cans of salty sardines stored in the pantry and picked tomatoes from the garden the caretaker tended.

He drank a lot of wine.

When the sun set, Ben locked himself in his room and slept. He slept long and hard, and he tried not to think about blood or gold or pretty girls with deadly fangs. He stayed in the primitive wing of the house with no electricity and let his phone die. When it was dark, he slept. When the sun rose, he woke.

Ben knew he'd have to go back to Los Angeles eventually, but he wanted to take some time to think about his life.

What the hell was he doing?

Who was he?

A human? A vampire in training? A lackey or a

leader?

Could he walk through a world where he was always seen as inferior because of his mortality? Would he be satisfied living in the human world again?

Was living in the human world even an option at this point?

Ben thought it would be Tenzin who found him eventually, but it was his uncle. Giovanni waited for him one morning a week or so after Ben had arrived in Tuscany, taking shelter in the library before Ben dragged himself out of bed.

His uncle said nothing at first. Then he stood, patted Ben's cheek, and said, "We'll talk tonight. I'm tired," before he left the room.

– ⊕ –

BEN took a nap that afternoon and woke to the smell of steak smoking on the grill. He walked out and saw Giovanni manipulating the flame around two thick cuts of beef, searing them from the outside before he warmed the coals underneath them and left the steaks on the grill to finish cooking. There was an open bottle of wine on the table and two full glasses.

"Sit," his uncle said. "The meat is almost done."

The dinner was simple, which was all he'd ever expect from Giovanni, who had not learned how to cook more than the basics in over five hundred years of life. Meat, bread, wine, and a few tomatoes sliced from the garden, with olive oil poured over them. Ben sat and drank his wine, staring out over the orchards at twilight.

Ben looked at his uncle.

Giovanni was, objectively speaking, the most handsome man Ben had ever seen. When he was in high school, all the girls had a crush on his Uncle Giovanni. Every girlfriend he'd brought home had angled for a hint of a smile. It had annoyed him until his last girlfriend said Ben and Giovanni looked more like brothers than uncle and nephew. That had made his chest puff up at the time, but now it freaked him out.

Because it was true. His uncle used clothes and hair and glasses to age himself for humans, but if you looked carefully, Giovanni didn't look a day over thirty. He'd stay that way forever, and Ben was quickly catching up.

"I talked with Tenzin in Rome," Giovanni said. "You have both made a friend in Emil Conti."

"Huh."

"The new regime in Naples is decidedly more open and willing to work with him. Added to that, they've already been able to shed more light on the library theft. Zeno was invited down examine the documents they were keeping from Emil's people. Emil believes Zeno's status as a native Neapolitan and former clergy will be of benefit in building trust."

"You must have agreed to let him go," Ben said. "He's under your aegis."

Giovanni drank some wine and shrugged. "It will help clear things up for my clients."

"Right."

"And Emil is a good ally. Filomena could be as well."

"She's something, all right."

Giovanni was silent.

"It's not that she used me," Ben said. "It's that I was oblivious to it. I thought I was a bishop when I was a pawn."

Giovanni nodded. "I understand. But you won't be oblivious next time."

"*If* there's a next time."

They were both silent for a long time.

"There doesn't have to be," Giovanni said. "Not for any of this. You know that, don't you?"

Ben cleared his throat. "Be honest. Has living a normal life ever really been an option for me?"

Giovanni paused. "I talked to Matt and Dez before I left."

"Yeah?" Ben sipped his wine. "How are they? I haven't been by for dinner in too long. How's Carina?"

"Growing quickly," Giovanni said with a smile. "She starts school in the fall. Soccer too. She already has her first set of cleats and her very own ball. It's purple. She's very excited."

Ben felt his throat close up. He remembered when Carina had been born. Had listened to her hummingbird heartbeat when Dez had been in the hospital in Rome. And now Carina was buying cleats and starting school.

His heart began to race. It was all happening too quickly. His uncle looked like his brother. Babies were growing up and Ben was graduating. Casper was slower every year, and Isadora's hearing was beginning to go.

"Gio—"

"I talked to Matt and Dez before I left LA," Giovanni said softly. "The apartment over their garage is empty right now. You could rent it if you wanted. Matt has an opening at the company in his online security division. You are more than qualified for it. You could—"

"It's not the job thing," Ben said in a rough voice. "I'm not worried about... It's not the job."

"I know." Giovanni stood and took the meat off the grill. "I know it's not about a job."

Giovanni sat down again and poured more wine while the meat rested and the temperature in the hills dropped. A cool breeze drifted over the tops of the trees, sending a shush of sound through the valley.

"Who am I?" Ben asked. "Benjamin Amir Rios, bastard pickpocket? Ben Vecchio, ward of the famous vampire? Your son? Tenzin's... butler?"

"You're none of those things," Giovanni said. "Or maybe you're a bit of all of them. What is important is that you have the choice." His uncle leaned across the table and squeezed his shoulder. "The man you are, Benjamin, the man you're becoming... I am privileged to know him. Whatever you choose—whatever you do—I will be there. Beatrice will be there. You are ours. Maybe you don't have our blood, but—"

"What if I wanted to be an immortal?"

Giovanni's hand tightened, and Ben realized for the first time how much his uncle truly wanted him to say yes.

"Either of us," Giovanni said. "You know this. Either of us would consider it a privilege to sire you."

Ben blinked hard. "And if I wanted to get an office job, find a nice wife, and raise fifteen kids?"

"I'd be godfather to every single one," Giovanni said. "And we would watch them always. Protect them always."

"Why are you making it so easy?" Ben sniffed.

"Because I love you. I want you to be happy."

Ben started to laugh. "And yet I hear a 'but.'"

"But I also want you to be challenged. Excited and driven about whatever you do. Because you won't be happy unless you're challenged."

Ben put his head in his hands and gripped his hair. "Why can't you just tell me what to do already?"

"It doesn't work that way."

"Sometimes I wish it did."

"No, you don't." Giovanni dropped a slab of steak on his plate and passed the bread. "Besides Ben, if I told you what to do, you'd find a way to do exactly the opposite. Then you'd argue with me that your way was what I should have chosen to begin with."

He took a deep breath. "Yeah, you're probably right."

"Of course I'm right. Now eat your dinner. I didn't ruin it this time."

"Thank God for small miracles."

THEY were kicking a ball back and forth the next night when Ben finally asked about her. "So did she go back to LA?"

Giovanni didn't need to ask whom he was talking about.

"I don't think so," he said. "She told me you needed human time."

Ben nodded.

"She also told me not to leave you alone too long because you're a brooder."

He rolled his eyes. "I'm fairly sure Tenzin thinks any reaction time over five minutes long is brooding."

Giovanni chuckled. "I'm not sure about that, but she does live in the moment."

"Has she always?"

"Well..." Giovanni stopped the ball with his foot. "You have to remember, she's the type of immortal that will get fed up with the world, then go sleep—figuratively speaking—in a cave for a century without thinking twice. So when she's awake, she's *present*."

Ben thought about that and it made an odd kind of sense.

"To get to be that age without going mad," Giovanni continued, "I think you have to live in the moment." Giovanni started kicking the ball again. "They're very different personalities, but if you think about Carwyn, he's the same way. He exists in the present. It's rare to get him ruminating about history. Vampires who ruminate about history tend to meet the sun because they become melancholy."

"You ruminate."

Giovanni nodded. "I used to. And how long do you think I would have lasted if I hadn't met Beatrice? Not long."

"Gio?"

"Hmm."

"Do you wonder? About me and Tenzin? About... whatever it is we are?"

Giovanni paused. "Not anymore. I love you both. Whatever you are... you'll figure it out, Ben. Both of you are simply more alive when you're together than when you're separate. I don't know what that means yet. I don't think you do either."

Ben let that one sink in for a while.

"It's okay," Giovanni said with a smile. "You don't have to know yet."

- ⊕ -

THEY were playing chess and drinking wine the following night.

"I think I want to move back to New York," Ben said.

Giovanni paused, a rook held in his hand. "You want the town house?"

"No," Ben said. "I'd stick out like a sore thumb in that neighborhood. I'm thinking about a loft in Brooklyn."

"For?"

Several kicks under the table from Fabi, a few dropped hints from Tenzin, and lots and lots of sleep were starting to make things clear. "I want to do what you do," Ben said. "Or at least I want to try. But not with books. I can't spend that much time looking for books, Gio. I'll go crazy."

"Do you think this is a surprise to me?"

"I want to find art," Ben said. "Antiquities. Take on clients and find things for them on commission. What do you think?"

Giovanni paused and finished his wine. It took three more moves from both of them before he replied.

"You can't do it alone," Giovanni said. "Not in the immortal world. No matter what your reputation, skills, or connections, there will be some who only take you seriously if you have a vampire partner."

"She'd go with me. You know she would."

"So you're the brains and Tenzin is the brawn?" Giovanni tapped the table. "It has possibilities. You'd be in O'Brien territory."

"Would that be a problem?"

"I don't think so. You don't have political ambitions, and neither does Tenzin. If you gave them a cut rate for family and associates like I do with Ernesto, you'd probably be fine. Cormac is the one to approach. Talk to Gavin."

Ben nodded, growing more and more excited about the idea as he thought about it. "I can do that."

"They wouldn't like Tenzin living there...," Giovanni said. "Or maybe they would. If it would open a business relationship with her allies in Asia, they might not have a problem. She'd have to play nice sometimes."

Ben shrugged. "I can get her to play nice when necessary."

"You're possibly the only one who can."

"Do you think it's a big enough market?" Ben asked.

"Could we make any money with it?"

"If you were good, you could make very good money, but we should consider it an offshoot of Beatrice's and my business to start. I'll refer clients to you when they need to find antiquities—"

"And eventually I'll refer clients to you if they need to find books."

Man and vampire both smiled.

"This could work, couldn't it, Gio?"

"Are you excited about the idea?"

Ben paused and really thought about it. "This feels right," he said. "More right than anything else I've thought of. I just have to keep Tenzin from forging copies of stuff we're hired to find."

Giovanni closed his eyes and turned back to the chessboard. "I'm pretending I didn't hear that."

"Good call."

"Don't do it again."

"I won't."

"You risk your reputation and mine, Benjamin."

"I get it. I get it. I'll keep her in line."

-✳︎-

TO Lady Filomena De Moura
Immortal Guardian of Naples and the Second
Parthenopean Republic

Nena (I told you I'd give you a nickname),

Forgive me for leaving your beautiful city so abruptly. I meant no offense, so I hope none was taken. The events that led to your rise were, admittedly, surprising to me, but I hope that Tenzin and I were able to assist you in our own way. I understand the collection of Sicilian tarì have been returned to the Neapolitan treasury. I am grateful that our small part in their recovery was satisfactory. (And the bonus was very much appreciated.)

As I have now discovered the delights of your city, I hope to return again soon. I understand you and Emil Conti are working toward smoother relations between the Neapolitan and Roman courts. I wish you both well.

Until our next meeting I remain...

Your admirer,
Benjamin Vecchio,
International Man of Mystery
Scourge of the _____ (still working on that one)

–✳–

DEAR Ben,

Come back to Naples soon. You will be welcome.

Nena

Epilogue

THE HUMIDITY WAS EVEN HIGHER than when he'd left two weeks before, but Ben was whistling when he saw the prow of Claudio's boat as it drew up to dock near the train station.

"*Ciao*, Claudio."

"*Ciao*, Ben."

He threw his satchel into the back of the boat and climbed in next to Claudio.

"It's still hot," Claudio said. "Even at night. It's not cooling off at all anymore."

"I know."

"You have your passport? Get it out. I'll take you to the airport right now. Get you out of this dreaded damp furnace."

"No, thanks."

Claudio shook his head. "Fine. Whatever you want. You're an idiot like her, I think. Come back in the spring. It's much nicer then."

Ben smiled. "You're the one who lives here, Claudio."

The young man shrugged. "Where else would I live? It's Venice. The greatest city in the world."

$$- \oplus -$$

BEN heard Louis's trumpet echoing down the quiet

canal as they approached the house. Claudio let him out at the end of the Rio Terà dei Assassini and tossed his bag up to him.

"You have the key?" Claudio asked.

Ben held it up. "I made my own copy."

"I'll talk to you later then. Try not to die."

Ben blinked. "Okay. Is there an ambush I need to know about?"

"No," Claudio said. "I say that to all the humans I know who hang out with vampires." He waved and drifted off down the canal.

Ben watched the lights of his boat until they disappeared around a corner, then he turned and punched in the gate code before he twisted the key in the lock. Both the gate and the door swung open easily because he'd oiled them before they left Venice the last time. It was little stuff like that Tenzin always forgot to do.

"Honey," he called quietly when he stepped into the courtyard. "I'm home."

A faint sound of laughter echoing off marble.

Ben dropped his bag on a bench and walked to the turntable at the end of the entry hall. He picked up the needle and skipped to "La Vie en Rose," then he walked over and plucked the wineglass out of Tenzin's hand and set it on the coffee table.

Accusing grey eyes met his. "I was drinking that."

"I know," he said. "But you should be dancing."

"This is becoming a bad habit, Benjamin."

Ben pulled her to her feet and spun her out before he tugged her back and grabbed her around the waist as the trumpet solo started. After a few minutes, she relaxed in his arms and let him lead.

"I thought you'd go back to LA," she said.

"I missed your house."

She chuckled. "Good to know where your loyalties are."

"My loyalties are never in question," he said in a soft voice. "You should know that by now."

She didn't say anything, but her hand gripped tighter at his waist.

They danced silently around the entry, their feet shuffling along the checkerboard marble as the record scratched and echoed and skipped. The moon rose through the arched window over the stairwell and the ancient house breathed with the tide.

Minutes of peaceful silence were broken when Ben groaned, "Why is it so *hot*?"

"Heat wave," Tenzin said. "They say it's the worst in sixty years."

"That's just hideous and wrong."

"And yet, you're still forcing me to dance."

"You like it."

"I don't—"

Ben slapped a hand over her mouth so she couldn't argue. "Stop. Just dance. It's Louis. We always dance to

Louis. That's the new rule." She bit his hand and he let go. "Ouch."

"It's so cute when you try to boss me around. Is this an absolute rule? What if a Louis Armstrong song happens to come on at an inopportune moment? If we're fighting for our lives, do we have to stop and dance?"

"We can be flexible in life-threatening situations."

The record switched to "Blueberry Hill," and they kept dancing.

"So," he said. "I did a lot of thinking in Tuscany."

"You brood."

"I was not..." He stopped talking so he didn't start yelling. *Take a deep breath.* "Thinking is not brooding. I was thinking."

"Fine. Whatever you say."

"And I figured out what you can call me when you introduce me."

Tenzin looked up, her eyes laughing. "Oh yes? Can I stick with life coach? That's my favorite so far. I was thinking about some other ones though—"

"No." Ben spun her round and round until she was laughing aloud. "I'm not going to be known as your life coach or your yoga instructor or your publicist."

"So what then?"

Tenzin took a wrong step and tried to take the lead, but Ben shook her arm until she stopped trying to push him around. "No. Don't do that, you'll just mess up the dance. Let me lead. I'm a better dancer."

"Fine." She relaxed and Ben stepped forward, dipping her until her hair brushed the ground.

He pulled her up. "Partner."

Tenzin blinked. "What?"

"You and I," he said, "are going to move to New York."

"Hmmm." It was a suspicious *hmmm*.

"We're going to find shiny, pretty things," Ben continued.

"I like that."

"And we're going to return them to the people paying us to find them."

"I don't like that so much."

"For a very generous fee."

Tenzin thought. She thought until the needle was bumping against the edge of the record, but Ben didn't stop dancing.

Finally, she asked, "Can we—?"

"No, we cannot make forgeries and keep the originals for ourselves."

She pouted. "You're no fun."

"I just need to know." Ben spun her out and tugged her back, the quiet lapping of the water in the canal the only accompaniment to their dance. "Are you in or out, Tenzin?"

Tenzin's eyes narrowed and the corner of her mouth turned up in a smile.

"In."

– ⊕ –

TENZIN let Ben turn the record over and dance with her for another half an hour.

She was glad she let him figure it out on his own. It was much more satisfying to know he'd come to the same conclusion she had years ago. It was obvious after their trip to China that he'd be the perfect partner to treasure hunt with her. It had taken him a little while to come around, but he couldn't help being slow. He was human.

For now.

THE END

Acknowledgements

I always have a long list of thank-yous when I travel, but for this trip, a few people definitely stood out. The staff at the Argentina Residenza in Rome and the AC staff in Venice were welcoming and incredibly informative. My most excellent tour guide in Naples and Pompeii, Fiorella Squillante, made our Naples experience a true pleasure and provided invaluable insight to this marvelous city.

Naples! Napoli, in general. Thank you. You are marvelous and I can't wait to visit you again.

Venice, my love. Despite your truly oppressive weather, I'll never turn down a chance to visit your magical streets.

A very special thank you to my Italian beta reader, Sara Villa, for her generous assistance and keen eyes.

Profuse thanks, as always, to my editors Lora Gasway and Anne Victory, my cover artists at Damonza, and my agents, Jane Dystel and Lauren Abramo.

And many thanks to my readers who have become such fans of this very unlikely (but oddly perfect) duo. Your love of these characters inspires me.

Also by Elizabeth Hunter

ELIZABETH HUNTER is a contemporary fantasy, paranormal romance, and paranormal mystery writer. She is a graduate of the University of Houston Honors College and a former English teacher. She once substitute taught a kindergarten class but decided that middle school was far less frightening. Thankfully, people now pay her to write books and eighth graders everywhere rejoice.

She currently lives in Central California with her son, two dogs, many plants, and a sadly empty fish tank. She is the author of the Elemental Mysteries and Elemental World series, the Cambio Springs series, the Irin Chronicles, and other works of fiction.

ElizabethHunterWrites.com

Made in the USA
San Bernardino, CA
19 March 2017